Dancing With An Angel

Sandy Loyd

DEDICATION

There are too many who have helped me on my path as a published author. I want to acknowledge my husband, who has always been my center. I also want to acknowledge other authors, Leslie Lynch and Caroline Fyffe whose advice help make the story better. And finally, to Pam Berehulke, my editor, who continually pushes me to become a better writer.

Thank you all.

Chapter 1

Where in the hell was the kid? Had his information been wrong?

Kyle Davidson checked his watch. Time was in short supply tonight. He had a date to keep.

Annoyed over how he'd gotten finagled into Maggie's plans in the first place, Kyle frowned. He should have known Grams's friend had something up her sleeve, and that her favor would hold objectionable strings.

In Maggie's defense, she had earned the favor fair and square, having spent six months babysitting his grandmother until she fully recovered from her stroke so he wouldn't have to hire a stranger. Kyle owed her a lot more than a few dates with a woman who wasn't supposed to know Maggie had set him up to ask her out.

The wind kicked up. Kyle shivered. He took a sip of tepid Starbucks coffee that had lost its warming effect, and continued to fret over the evening to come.

Grams and Maggie had obviously gotten together. Done some scheming, along with a little matchmaking. He knew damn well he shouldn't let the two women he cared most about in his life get away with such manipulations. Hell, he wasn't even sure this Mary Ann Murphy would go out with him.

Pride made him take on the challenge, and pride wouldn't let him back out of it. How stupid was that?

He rubbed his right thigh after squatting for another ten minutes. Blood had surely quit circulating to his toes. The sun had long set and it was colder than average for a mid-November evening. Kyle stood, shook each foot to bring back the feeling, and checked his watch. Then he sat back on his haunches and refocused on the car centered under the street light.

Thank God it wasn't raining.

Movement from the corner drew his gaze. A lanky kid, not even a teenager yet according to his mother, stepped into view. Angelo Rodriguez looked too young and innocent to be making his initiation into the Cutthroats, a gang Kyle had been waging war on since a few members had mugged and robbed his grandmother two years earlier. It was the same gang his Little Brother, Rico Gonzalez, had belonged to before he'd been shot and killed in a drug bust gone bad. Kyle had worked hard to be the type of mentor to Rico the Big Brothers program required. Unfortunately, one or two get-togethers a week didn't compensate for a bad home environment. Kids from the inner city needed a place to become strong enough to withstand the allure of easy money and acceptance the Cutthroats provided.

Angelo, AKA Ziggy, cautiously made his way to the Nissan 370Z, the bait Kyle had parked half an hour earlier.

Shaking his head, Kyle tossed his to-go cup into a nearby trash bin and silently slid out from behind his hiding spot. Unfortunately, Ziggy turned at the wrong moment. The kid spotted him and sprang into a run.

Prepared, Kyle sprinted after him and within seconds grabbed the hood of his gangland sweatshirt. Reeling back from having his momentum interrupted, Ziggy squirmed like a cat held over water.

His grip firm, Kyle inhaled deeply a couple of times to catch his breath, then tsk-tsked. "You know if you weren't wearing this hoodie, you might have gotten away."

"Shove it, asshole." Ziggy's fierce look would have stopped a bulldozer head-on, but considering the boy's rapid heartbeat and red face, it was all bluff. "I ain't done nothing wrong."

Kyle smiled. "So, what? I'm supposed to wait around for you to screw up the locks on my car when you try to steal it? Do I have *stupid* carved into my forehead?" According to Ms. Rodriguez, Angelo was a good kid who got in with a bad crowd. Exactly like Rico. Kyle wasn't about to let anyone he could help get sucked in too. Not without giving it a one-hundred-percent effort.

"I was just lookin' at it, mister." The kid had that belligerent attitude down pat as he added, "That ain't no crime, is it?"

"Right." Kyle nodded to the tool in the boy's hand. "You should know that even if you got inside, the keyless starter is beyond your ability." Lucky for him, the kid was too new at the game to realize his mistake.

"I told ya. I was mindin' my own business. Wasn't gonna hot-wire no car."

"Save it for someone who cares." Kyle continued dragging him by the hood he'd twisted to prevent escape. At the passenger side of the Z, he hit the silver button on the door, opened it, and shoved the kid inside.

No easy feat with Ziggy still thrashing about, doing his damnedest to get loose. Holding him in place with one hand on his chest, Kyle grabbed his arm to secure it with a zip tie, making sure the kid's hand wouldn't slip out of it. He then strung in another tie and looped it through a ring he'd added to the frame for the express purpose of keeping kids like him from bolting out of the car. Kyle slammed the door and ran around to the driver's side.

"Where're you taking me?" Ziggy asked in a tone surpassing twelve on the one-to-ten attitude scale, but he couldn't keep the fear out of his eyes.

Kyle smiled. "You'll see." It would probably be best if he didn't mention the ranch for wayward boys out in the middle of the valley. Angelo Rodriguez would soon find out he'd be stuck there long enough to learn some manners, as well as some grammar.

"You can't just kidnap me. I know my rights."

"As a minor, your rights are limited," Kyle said, wondering how the boy, who shook like a leaf, kept up such an affronted attitude. "Let's say I own your ass for the time being." Ziggy was in his protective custody for the next six months.

"Are you a cop? You can't arrest me when I ain't done nothing wrong. I'll sue!"

"With what?" Kyle glanced at him. "Money you make stealing cars for the Cutthroats?"

"Does my momma know about this?" Ziggy had lost some of his swagger. His voice cracked a bit.

"She signed the paperwork, which means you're stuck with me, kid." Kyle had his mother's permission to keep the boy as long as it took to turn him around and give him alternatives to joining a gang.

Ziggy slumped in the seat. "There'll be hell to pay when my gang hears about this."

Kyle grunted. "You really think they'll step in to save your ass when you haven't proven yourself?"

The f-bombs flying out of Ziggy's mouth, mixed in with how much Kyle had screwed up his life, would have caused a hardened criminal to flinch. "Now I gotta find some way to save face."

"What if you had another alternative?"

"I'm smart enough to know if I can't beat 'em, I might as well join 'em, cuz there ain't no other way when you live where I live."

Wasn't that the truth. No different than Rico. "At least give the place I'm taking you to a chance."

Ziggy rolled his eyes, his expression saying *No effing way* as if he were shouting. Then he crossed his arms, or crossed them as much as his restraint allowed. "Do-gooders like you just mess our lives up more."

Another true statement. The overburdened system created to help needy children only compounded the problem, and made their lives worse for too many.

"Look," Kyle said. "All I'm asking for is a chance. It's something your momma wants for you. She doesn't want to have to identify your dead body like she did your cousin, Paulo."

The rest of Ziggy's bravado fractured and fell piece by piece, unmasking a face full of agony. "I planned to kill a few rat-bastard Dragons," he said, naming a rival gang. "The only way I can do that is to become a Cutthroat." His shoulders slumped in defeat. "And you're just gettin' in my way."

"More than likely you'll get yourself killed. What will happen to your momma then?" When Ziggy remained silent, he added, "What if there really is a better way?"

The kid threw out a disbelieving snort and did another eye roll.

"How about by using your brains and doing something with your life?"

That got his attention. "Like what?"

"Like getting an education and becoming a better person. There are a hundred things you could do to avenge Paulo's death, but the worst is to die too young yourself." Kyle sighed. "Give it a chance. You really have no choice, so you might as well sit back and enjoy the ride."

The boy mulled that over for a moment, then nodded as he took in the dashboard. "This *is* a rad car, man."

A satisfied smile tugged to break free. Ziggy's momma had it right. He simply needed to steer the boy in the right direction.

"Man oh man, this baby can fly."

Looking over, Kyle nodded. "She sure can." Because he was in a hurry to make his date, every now and then when he checked the speedometer, he was speeding. He had to work at staying within the speed limit. Catching Ziggy in the act had taken longer than anticipated.

When he reached his destination, the clock on the dashboard read 7:05.

Kyle cut the restraints holding the boy and helped him out of the car. If he hurried, he could still make the forty-five-minute

4

drive to the church hall in time to play the first round of bingo with his grandmother, and meet this paragon Maggie was so fixated on.

"What is this place?" Ziggy did a complete three-sixty, looking totally lost and more like the twelve-year-old boy he was rather than the punk he'd tried to emulate earlier.

"It's your new home. In a few months you'll thank me. But for a while, you'll be wishing I were dead." Keeping a firm grip on the boy's arm, he headed toward the entrance. There was nowhere to run, but he had no intention of wasting more time chasing him down if the kid decided to risk it.

"Hey, Holly," Kyle said to the no-nonsense woman at the check-in desk. Holly Thomas, the head of admissions, ran the place. She had her own reasons for being here, just as Kyle had his for starting A Leg Up For Kids. After five years, he didn't know what he'd do without her.

"So, you must be Angelo." She held a clipboard with the boy's admission forms. "It's nice to meet you. I'm Holly."

Thank God the paperwork had been done two days ago. Knowing the kid was now in good hands, Kyle hurried toward the exit, leaving Ziggy with Holly as a string of profanities followed him out the door. Ziggy sure had a colorful vocabulary.

The Z purred like a kitten as he sped west. Hopefully he could make it to bingo before the first round started. Otherwise, this Mary Ann chick would think it strange he'd even bothered to show up at all. Or she'd guess his true reason for being there. Maggie had warned him that if Mary Ann sensed a setup, she'd run for the hills. Then all bets were off, and he'd have to do something else to pay Maggie back.

At least this way, he'd meet a nice girl and have a few fun dates. Not that he couldn't find nice girls on his own. However, most women he met knew of his background. Kyle was never sure if women went out with him due to his bank balance or because they liked him. He wasn't naive enough after Andrea to believe money didn't play a big part.

***

The SuperSavMart door opened automatically and Mary Ann Murphy started inside. She swore under her breath after noticing the guy a few feet in front of her heading for the exit. Steve Henderson was the one person in the whole world she could go her entire life without seeing and then die happy.

Even worse, Mrs. Steve Henderson was right behind him. Mary Ann knew this because their wedding had been announced in the newspapers, about the same time she stopped reading the society section. Steven and Taylor Henderson were the closest things to celebrities in San Mateo, California. Taylor was the granddaughter of a Donald Trump-like guy who owned ten percent of the real estate in San Mateo. San Mateo wasn't New York or San Francisco, but the property he owned was worth a ton of money. In Mary Ann's mind, money tended to make celebrities of otherwise uninteresting people.

"Excuse us." Steve stepped aside at the same time he reached for his wife's arm. Unfortunately, Mary Ann hadn't been able to step past him fast enough before he said in a loud voice, "Mary Ann? I can't believe it! How are you?"

Mary Ann just smiled, the same one she reserved for the oral surgeon about to perform a root canal. "Steve. It's great to see you," she lied. "And you must be Steve's wife." Her smile became more strained as she clenched her teeth harder. "So nice to meet you." Another blatant lie. Hopefully God would not strike her down, seeing as how she was on her way to meet her mom and a group of her friends for church bingo. But God had to understand how she felt and would forgive her, even without going to confession. She stuck out her hand.

Taylor's handshake was like overdone pasta—limp. But the woman didn't need a firm handshake with her megabucks. After all, that's how she'd landed Steve.

"Are you the one who makes jewelry and sells it out of her house?" the woman asked, as if that were somehow a tacky endeavor.

"Yes. As a matter of fact, these are a couple of my pieces." She held up her hand to show off her latest designs that were quickly becoming best sellers among her clientele. "I moved into my own showroom a few months ago."

"How nice." Taylor did well to hide her smirk, but the eye roll was impossible to miss.

"They're best sellers. And you know what they say about customers?" When Taylor's gaze turned questioning, Mary Ann smiled sweetly. "They're always right." She earned her living the hard way. By working, something Taylor most likely knew nothing about.

"What brings you to Hayward?" Not that she really cared, but at least it shifted the focus from her business, one barely meeting its payroll. But it was hers, and at least her customers liked the bracelets she made.

"We needed more room." Steve turned to his wife and grinned. "We're just across the bridge from my office in San Mateo." He paused. "How about you?"

"I moved to be closer to my family." Another blatant lie. The rents were cheaper on the east side of the bay, but she'd die before she'd admit it.

Damn, how nice it would be to fling her success in Steve's face along with some rich guy she was dating. Even a starving artist would work. Mary Ann thought she'd overcome his rejection, but after actually coming face-to-face with him, she knew that was another lie.

Steve's main reason for dumping her was as bogus as a Gucci knockoff. He wasn't ready to settle down. Right. It only took him a few months to meet and marry Taylor and her megabucks. More likely having a nobody for a wife, whose dad toiled as a laborer, didn't look good on a résumé.

"How is the family?" Steve asked as if he really cared, when the jerk had never bothered to learn any of her siblings' names.

"Fine." It was then that Mary Ann actually paid more attention to the stroller.

She did a recount. Had the earth tilted on its axis? Steve Henderson had actually gone forth and multiplied? With triplets?

"How precious," she said, too stunned to say anything else, and trying not to melt at the sight of three sweet infants wearing identical outfits but in different colors.

Once her equilibrium returned, Mary Ann glanced back up at him. Here Steve had called her a pre-made baby maker, and look who was calling the kettle black. She offered another phony smile. "Congratulations. You certainly had me fooled." Filled with a need to escape, she scooted past them. "You'll have to excuse me, I'm running late." Then she turned and strode with purpose down the first aisle without looking back.

At the frozen foods, she stopped and leaned her head against the cool freezer, hoping to quell the heat of embarrassment and anger from overtaking her. Damn the man. Why did he have to look so good? But then why wouldn't he with his fifty-dollar haircut and thousand-dollar suit? She only had to remember he was a toad and probably made Taylor have liposuction after the babies

7

were born. Either that or she had great genes. Mary Ann glanced down at her body, feeling dowdy and overweight compared to the sleek Taylor Henderson. Crossing her arms to cover her ample breasts, she wished her figure were more sleek than the hourglass shape she'd inherited from her mom. Now in her fifties, her mother hadn't lost her figure, but there was no mistaking the fact that she'd had nine kids. Colleen Murphy looked matronly. And happy, Mary Ann added mentally.

She hurried through the store to locate the daubers for the bingo cards her mother had asked her to pick up, but her thoughts remained on the man who'd once called her a baby-making machine. Steve's actions and comments had hurt her to the core. He'd done a number on her in more ways than one, and she'd let him. She needed to give herself permission to grieve for what could have been. She hadn't been lacking in anything. He had.

For a solid year after their breakup, Mary Ann had pretended to be a party girl and had gone through the motions of dating. The truth was, she didn't trust her judgment and kept all guys at a distance. She sure as heck never wanted to experience more heartache.

Mary Ann found the daubers in the school supply section, grabbed a handful, and headed for the check-out stand. Thankfully, there was no sign of the Hendersons.

Once in her car, she shoved all thoughts of Steve and his cute little family from her brain. But damn it all, her traitorous heart shouted. *That should have been me.*

Chapter 2

Mary Ann found an empty spot way in the back. Judging by the crowded parking lot, church bingo was popular in Maggie McAllister's neighborhood. Last week, the group had played at her mother's parish church. Thanks to her run-in with Steve, Mary Ann would barely make it in time to find a place to sit before the games started. In a hurry, she climbed out of the car, hit the keypad, and practically sprinted to the entrance, slowing only when she reached the door.

As predicted, the church rec hall that doubled as a bingo parlor on Friday nights was packed. Players intent on winning had their good luck charms lined up in front of them. Mary Ann searched the room, wondering where they bought the troll dolls, the obvious charm of the month. Thank God smoking wasn't allowed, because she could just imagine these diehards with cigarettes hanging out of their mouths as they played.

"Yoo-hoo! We're over here, dear."

Mary Ann recognized the voice and glanced in its direction, spotting the table of six women and one man, who seemed as out of place as a straitlaced guy in a biker bar. He looked too clean-cut, not the type to wear leather and chains, and she'd bet money if he took off his shirt, there'd be no tattoos marking his well-toned upper body. Her kind of guy. She never understood why anyone would cover muscled arms and chests with ink. Why mess with perfection?

The empty chair next to him was obviously for her. That didn't bode well. At least the guy looked like he could carry on a conversation. Better yet, he was a hunk. She pushed the last half hour out of her thoughts and headed toward them. Her evening just got more entertaining.

If this guy was willing to sit with a bunch of old ladies, he had to be a decent sort, even if her mom had something to do with his presence tonight. What could it hurt to flirt a little and have some fun? Maybe it would get her mom and Maggie off her back about finding a good man and settling down. After seeing Steve with family in tow, she didn't need any reminders of her single status.

"Here you go, Mom." Mary Ann handed her the daubing markers that before her foray into bingo she had no idea existed. Yet every person present had at least one.

"Bless you, girl," Blanche Llewellyn said in a British accent, reaching for a green marker. "The ink is running dry on this and I feel like a winner tonight." Blanche tossed the one she'd been holding into a nearby trash can with the precision of a pro basketball player, then eagerly started daubing the free spots on the several sheets in front of her. "Wouldn't want to miss any of my numbers." The elderly lady was from Wales and was always quick to point out that while Wales was part of the United Kingdom, it was separate from England. In Mary Ann's mind, it was a lot like a Texan claiming no relation to an Oklahoman, even though both areas were similar and part of the United States. Unless a person actually lived in those places, they'd never know the difference. Even their accents were similar to the uninformed ear.

Mary Ann acknowledged the other women she knew at the table with a nod. Both Mrs. Bechelli and Maggie greeted her with smiles. Mary Ann turned to Vickie Collins, her best friend's mom, who stood and gave her a quick hug. "Where's Sam?" she asked.

"She had a deadline to meet with one of her clients. Something about a design change on the plans for his building, so she had to cancel."

Stifling a surge of disappointment, she pulled out the empty chair to sit. Damn. Sam had promised to be here, which was the only reason she'd agreed to attend tonight. She'd pay Sam back for this. The thought dissipated as Maggie said, "Glad you could make it, Mary Ann. This is a good friend, Irma Davidson. Her grandson, Kyle, took Sam's place."

The older woman stretched a hand out in front of her grandson's chest. "Nice to meet you," she said smiling. "Call me Irma."

After releasing her hand, Mary Ann then turned to Irma's grandson and got caught in the most beautiful green gaze. It should be a crime for a man to have eyes like that, she thought, trying not to gawk. When she realized he also had a hand out, she took it. A burst of energy zapped her, sending a tingling sensation up her arm, reminding her of the time she'd unplugged a frayed cord only to receive a shock that nearly dropped her to her knees. His startled expression told her he'd felt a similar reaction.

"What did you say your name was?" she was able to get out when she could finally speak without letting the entire room know her world had tilted on its axis twice in one night.

"Kyle. Kyle Davidson." He had a gorgeous smile to go with those eyes.

She glanced at Irma, noting her in more detail. The little gray-haired lady had a fragile look about her, as if a stiff wind could blow her away. Yet there was nothing fragile about that steely gaze zeroed in on her. Those assessing eyes were disturbing, so much so that Mary Ann looked down to make sure her sweater wasn't stained and that it covered all the necessary parts.

"Here're your sheets, Mary Ann," her mother said, handing her a short stack of bingo cards. "They're about to begin. Good thing we were able to save you a seat."

"I had to work late, then I had to stop to get the daubers." Mary Ann cleared her throat, trying to calm her racing pulse. Wouldn't do for the heartthrob sitting next to her to realize how much he affected her. Not that she really cared, but she hadn't refreshed her makeup and probably looked as pale as a ghost. If she'd known about him earlier, she'd have also changed into something besides jeans and sweater.

Kyle reached out to snag a marker.

Startled, she leaned back. As she inhaled, his spicy scent wafted under her nose, adding to her awareness of him.

He must have noted her response because he grinned and moved closer, causing her to stretch farther back in her seat.

"What?" He sniffed under each arm. "Do I have BO or something?"

Her eyes grew big as she met his gaze. When she realized he was teasing her, she laughed. "No. It's not every day I get to sit next to eye candy while playing bingo."

His grin widened. "Eye candy, huh?" He winked and added, "Any time you want to take a nibble, just let me know."

Blanche, on the other side of the table, cackled. "That's cute, hon. I'll have to remember that when I talk to Ralph."

Her mother angled toward her and whispered, "Ralph is the man at her assisted living area she's trying to seduce."

"Mother!"

"Well, it's true. And I don't know why you're all upset. You've always laughed at Blanche's jokes in the past."

Mary Ann's cheeks flamed. She could easily joke about nibbling, sex, and seductions with them but with Kyle present, it was another matter. "You don't have to broadcast it to the entire room." Too afraid to look at the man next to her, she kept her gaze plastered to the table in front of her, wishing she could disappear.

Colleen looked at Kyle. "She *does* know where babies come from, I promise you." When Mary Ann rolled her eyes, her mother ignored her and turned to Blanche. "So, how's that going?"

"He's shy and says he likes to be the one to take control. Hell, if I waited for him to make the first move, I'd be dead and buried. I plan on getting a little more action before the Lord takes me."

Mary Ann shook her head, wondering if Kyle thought he'd entered some kind of twilight zone.

"Oh, come on, sweetie, lighten up," her mother said, catching her gaze. "We're merely having fun. Usually you're the first one cracking jokes."

Yeah, she usually was, especially with this group. But those times didn't include a Jake Gyllenhaal look-alike sitting next to her. Deciding to go with the flow, she shucked her embarrassment and turned to Kyle. "I'm amazed you're so gutsy. I don't think you realize what you've gotten yourself into by agreeing to play at this table. Are you sure you want to stay?"

That killer smile was back. Worse, it extended all the way to those eyes. "That's a good enough reason right there."

Confused, she scrunched her forehead.

"I strive to amaze beautiful women."

Blanche cackled again. "Damn, I should be sitting over there where I can hear better. I've picked up more good lines in ten minutes than I've heard in a year."

Kyle chuckled. "I couldn't resist."

Mary Ann laughed, trying not to think about how boring her love life was, that being here tonight with a bunch of older women was the highlight of her week, or that his presence had added an element of excitement she'd never expected. "Don't listen to Blanche. She knows more pickup lines than George Clooney."

Blanche sighed dreamily. "Now there's one hell of a man I wouldn't mind being stranded on a beach with."

"You wouldn't know what to do with someone like him. Besides, a beach is the worst place to make love," Mrs. Bechelli said, finally piping up. "Sand gets everywhere and it's the dickens to get it out."

Mary Ann turned to Kyle. "See what I mean?" She grinned when his stunned gaze moved around the table. "You ladies should ease up tonight. Kyle obviously isn't used to such candor."

"No, don't stop." He put up a hand. "It's just getting interesting."

She glanced at his fingers. Rough and calloused, unlike good ol' Steve's. Her ex had never done a bit of hard labor in his life. Kyle had the hands of someone who wasn't afraid to get dirty. That kind of man she could understand and deal with on an equal footing. After all, she knew how to work hard. Intrigued with how his hands fit with the rest of him, she eyed him and asked, "So, what do you do, Kyle?" She smiled and brushed a dark strand behind her ears. "When you're not playing bingo?"

"I'm in construction."

The man at the podium banged his gavel, leaving her no more time for reflection about his answer. "We're about to begin calling out numbers." He went on to explain the game and Mary Ann rolled her eyes. The room was full of diehard bingo players who needed no instruction. Finally, he ended with, "Has everyone covered their free spaces?" A murmur of yeses rose up.

"Good. Then let's play bingo." He nodded to the lady next to him, who pulled a lever and a ball bounced up. She then handed it to the caller. "The first number is G-75."

After he called out half a dozen numbers, her mother pointed to Mary Ann's sheet. "Oh, look!" she said in a loud voice that carried in the noisy room. "You only need one more space and you're a winner."

Mary Ann smiled. Her mother was actually more excited over the thought of her daughter winning something than she was.

When B-12 was called out, Colleen Murphy shrieked, "You won!" at the same time Mary Ann yelled, "Bingo." A sense of enthusiasm filled her. In the six months since she'd started playing with these crazy women, Mary Ann had never won. Until now.

The announcer grinned. "Well, come on up, little lady." He waited until she stood in front of him before he added, "As announced earlier, our prize for the first round is six ballroom dancing lessons."

"Thanks." She took the envelope he handed her, trying hard not to show her disappointment. What in the hell was she going to do with ballroom dancing lessons?

Once back at the table, she said as much to the group as she sat.

"Maybe I can sell them."

"I'd take them off your hands," Blanche offered. "But my arthritis is kicking up lately. Besides, Carl uses a walker and I doubt he'd be interested, and he'd be affronted if I took someone else."

Colleen sighed. "It'd be such a shame not to use them when I know you'd love to learn. You've said as much during *Dancing with the Stars*."

Mary Ann groaned. Why not tell the whole world her silly fantasy? "Well gee, Mom, dancing requires a partner." Something she lacked.

"Don't be silly. I'm sure you can find someone among the dozen or so you've been dating."

Oh, great! Now Colleen was making her out to be some kind of Jezebel or man-eater. What would her mother think if she knew few of those men made it past the second date? Mary Ann didn't take sex lightly. Most got their walking papers at that point because they expected sex by the third date. The few who didn't, rarely made it to a fourth. After Steve, she'd become rather picky. No one from the group of guys she'd dated lately interested her enough to warrant a fifth date.

"I can't think of anyone I'd like to ask," she murmured to her mother, sending her a pointed look.

Instead of taking the hint, Colleen said, "I bet Kyle would take you, wouldn't you?"

Mary Ann wanted to crawl under the table. She turned to Kyle, who only shrugged. "Sure. Sounds like fun," he said, despite being put on the spot.

Her mom practically clapped her hands. "Then it's decided. Kyle will make a perfect partner."

Just as she was about to argue, the announcer banged his gavel, ready to start calling the numbers for another game. Colleen shushed her. "We'll discuss it later. I want to hear the numbers."

"I'm winning this next round," Maggie said. "I feel lucky, too."

In silence, Mary Ann shook her head and went back to the game. She'd talk to Kyle, well away from this nosy group, and let him know she didn't expect him to take lessons with her.

Maybe Jimmy Rae, her gay next-door neighbor, would like to learn. Problem was, she had a sneaking suspicion he'd want her to lead and she'd have to learn the male steps, which would be useless. If worse came to worst, she could give both tickets to him. At least they wouldn't go to waste. Jimmy Rae loved watching

Dancing with the Stars as much as she did.

Thankful the group at the table was more interested in the sheets in front of them than her love life, Mary Ann played several rounds in peace.

"That's it until after dinner is over, folks," the announcer said. "Enjoy your meal. But don't go away. We still have blackout bingo to go, and our jackpot for the night is up to two hundred dollars."

No one else at their table had won.

Mary Ann bit back a smile when Blanche wadded up the latest sheet and grumbled an indelicate retort. She hadn't realized the lady even knew a word like that, much less how to use it.

It was even harder to keep a straight face when the others joined in with complaints about their losing streak. Mrs. Bechelli had even paid for two dinners to get twice as many sheets.

These women took their bingo seriously and expected to win.

Mary Ann rose and pushed in her chair. She turned and almost bumped into Kyle, who appeared to be waiting for her. Probably to offer an excuse as to why he couldn't take lessons. Well, *I'll simply beat him to the punch,* she thought, pasting a warm smile on her face.

Chapter 3

Kyle appreciated the view of Mary Ann's jeans-clad backside as she made her way through the food line in front of him. When she turned, surprising him, he dragged his gaze northward, making a concerted effort not to pause too long on her snug sweater, outlining a figure no red-blooded male could ignore.

"Look," she said, offering an apologetic smile. "I realize dancing isn't a guy's thing, so you're off the hook."

"What do you mean?" Kyle hadn't expected her to try to back out. He damn sure wasn't going to make it easy for her.

She pushed a strand of hair behind her ear. "I mean that was an obvious setup."

"Oh?" His gaze lingered on Mary Ann's smile.

"Yeah." An unladylike snort erupted from her sexy mouth.

A mouth Kyle had to quit thinking about kissing. Most annoying, since he didn't normally have those kinds of thoughts around women he'd just met. Especially now that he'd sworn off dating.

"My mother and Maggie had to have cooked this up." Her voice held a note of conviction and pulled his focus higher.

"No way. You won the round fair and square." How had Mary Ann caught on to their shenanigans so quickly? Should he tell her his part in this? Turning, he fastened his gaze on the group of ladies in the line behind them as his mind churned. When Maggie offered a too-smug smile, he swore under his breath. It meant something. Yeah...that the older woman was crafty like a fox.

Dancing lessons would be a great way to pay his debt to Maggie for taking such good care of Grams, all without Mary Ann knowing he was involved from the beginning. Still, he couldn't dismiss the idea that this was more than a simple debt repayment, or that he was as much a pawn in their game as she was. It was his own fault for jumping at her offer and not asking questions first.

"There's no possible way they could finagle the right random numbers to come up." Even as he stated the fact, more doubt resurfaced. Was the entire congregation in on it too? He had a hard time buying that. "Besides, it's just dancing. If you can handle my two left feet, I can handle a few classes." Sure, he was attracted to Mary Ann, but he could manage attraction.

When Grams caught him watching her, she smiled and waved. A sense of mischievousness in her expression clanged the warning bell in his brain louder. They were good; he'd give them that. But were they *that* good?

"Maybe so, but you don't have to get sucked into their schemes," Mary Ann said, drawing his attention back to her lips. "Learning to ballroom dance is one of my dreams, and I'm actually excited about the classes, but I can talk a friend into taking them with me."

Despite sensing a noose closing around his neck, he dipped his head. "I'd really like to learn too." He'd keep things light and under control. That way he'd avoid any likely traps if Maggie and Grams were up to setting them. "It'll be fun."

Mary Ann eyed him suspiciously. Even her smile looked skeptical. "Really?"

Kyle cast a brief glance at the ladies before refocusing on Mary Ann. "Yeah, really!"

In a bold move, she perused the length of him, starting at his eyes, moving slowly toward his shoes and back up again, in a most suggestive manner. He couldn't help but respond when her gaze ended where it began, locking stares with him. Her friendly smile did strange things to his insides as she released his gaze. "Okay. If you say so." She turned to follow the person in front of her. "But I expect you to go the whole nine yards," she said over her shoulder. "No quitting in the middle."

Presenting a sly smile, he made an *X* on his chest and her soft laughter floated back. "Cross my heart. I'll endure every last minute."

At the front of the line, she grabbed a plate of the worst-looking sloppy joes Kyle had ever seen, next to mushy green beans. He sighed. Forty bucks for this dinner, which included the sheets to play bingo, so it wouldn't be called gambling? He'd much rather pay the full amount for the sheets and forgo the fine cuisine. That way the church would save the money they'd put into buying and fixing the food. Then everyone would be happy, except the bureaucrats who created stupid rules about fundraising in the first place.

Or maybe I was wrong, he thought, glancing around. The parishioners all seemed to be enjoying their dinner. Maybe it tasted better than it looked. One could only hope.

He sprang for drinks because it was an obvious money-maker. The British lady had brought her own, which amused Kyle. Too bad they couldn't charge by the game sheet. That would make a ton of money, judging from the bingo sharps at his table. He'd never seen anything like it. Who knew a simple bingo game could bring out the gambling beast in these women.

When the meal was over, the blackout game proceeded in earnest. Kyle caught Mary Ann's gaze several times during the game, and it was obvious from the amused glimmer in her hazel eyes, now more blue than gray, she was on his wavelength.

When the round ended and no one at their table won, the ladies stood, collecting their belongings. Before Mary Ann could get away, Kyle stopped her. "Wait a minute and I'll walk you to your car."

"Are you coming, Mom?" She glanced at her mother.

"No, Vickie's giving me a ride, so you go on. I'll be fine."

Mary Ann turned back to him. "Proceed to walk me at your own risk because I have a feeling it's all part of their evil plan. Don't let it be said that I never warned you about how cunning these ladies can be."

Kyle lifted a brow. "That sounds like a challenge."

She laughed.

The vibration of it zinged through his ears, making a beeline to his gut. Damn, if she didn't have a sexy laugh.

Out in the parking lot quickly emptying of cars, she pointed. "I'm way over there."

His gaze followed her finger, where a lone Camry was parked in the very last row.

Side by side, they started in that direction, walking slowly.

As they neared her car, he stopped. "Look, I know we just met, but..." Noting her guarded expression, he cleared his throat. "It's still early." He glanced at his watch. "Only ten thirty. If you're game, I know a place not far from here that serves decent wines along with some tempting desserts."

She stuck her hands in her jeans pockets, rocked back on her heels, and studied his face, as if trying to figure him out.

He held up his hands. "No strings. Just a sugary treat and one glass of wine. Or coffee, if you'd prefer." She wasn't at all what he expected and that intrigued him. He didn't know one woman her age who would sit for two hours with a bunch of elderly bingo hounds and do so in such an enjoyable manner.

Mary Ann caught several strands of hair that blew in the wind and pushed them behind her ear, an endearing habit he'd seen her do half a dozen times during the last two hours. Every time she'd done it, the motion had drawn his attention to her hair. Now, as then, he had to squelch the urge to run his fingers through those lush dark tresses to see if they were as soft as they looked.

"Come on," he said. "I'll drive and drop you back at your car afterward."

She glanced at the hand he still had out. Then her gaze took a trip north to his eyes. Her eyebrows arched. "How do I know you're not some serial killer who uses bingo and old ladies to perpetrate a con in order to kidnap me?"

Kyle laughed. "Is that what you really think?"

"No." Her voice trailed off. "But you must admit it seems a little reckless. After all, I did just meet you and know nothing about you other than you work in construction and have a grandmother named Irma, and you expect me to walk hand in hand with you to your car and get inside and trust that you'll do as you say."

"Are you feeling reckless tonight?" he asked flirtatiously, unable to look away. Those unusual hazel eyes were definitely a window with an ample view of her thoughts.

"And if I said yes," she answered in a throaty whisper. "What would you do?" Her question was a challenge, which along with the invitation now shining in her eyes, tugged on his self-restraint.

His focus zeroed in on her lips. He smiled. In slow motion, he took a step and leaned closer. Giving her plenty of time to back away, he stopped an inch from her face. "I'd have to admit to feeling a little reckless myself." He grazed her mouth with the barest of pressure. Once. Twice. Three times. And still she didn't move. Then his arms went around her and he gave in to the temptation dogging him since the first moment she'd warned him about the women at the table. God, she tasted like sunshine and raindrops and sugar and vinegar and heaven and hell combined. Despite the contrasts—or maybe because of them—he deepened the kiss.

"Get a room."

The yell and honk from a passing car broke into his thoughts. Shit! He hadn't expected the kiss to escalate at all, never mind how

19

quickly it did. Immediately, he dropped his hands and broke their connection by stepping back.

Kyle swallowed hard and ran a hand through his hair. How in the hell had he lost track of where they were? Kissing in a church parking lot, for Christ's sake.

Glancing around, he noted they were relatively alone. Thank God for small favors. If the bingo ladies had seen them, no telling how they'd interpret the last few minutes, but they'd probably take the credit.

"I can certainly see your dilemma," Kyle finally said once he found his voice. Rubbing his neck with his right hand, he kept his gaze fastened on the ground. "I can't say I'm sorry for that because I'm not. If I were you, I'd steer clear." He should take his own advice because he liked kissing her. Way too much.

Mary Ann laughed, grabbed his free hand, and started walking. "Good thing you're not me, because I rather liked what just happened."

Left with no choice but to follow her, he did. He risked a peek in her direction as they passed under a streetlight. Amusement sizzled in her expressive eyes, aided by another saucy smile. "Aren't you worried I'll kidnap you and take you back to my dungeon?"

"No." Her smile morphed into a more calculating one and Mary Ann shook her head. "You're a nice guy."

"Ouch!" Kyle slowed and pretended to clutch at his chest. "That's not something any guy wants to hear." After straightening, he glanced at her lips again. "I almost prefer being thought of as a serial killer who abducts his prey and takes her back to his castle."

She halted in midstride and turned his way. "I don't do castles until at least the tenth date."

"But this is not a date, remember? And there are only six dance lessons."

She let go of his hand to run the back of her fingers down the side of his face. He struggled not to react or move a muscle as she patted his cheek. The half dozen bracelets on her wrist jangled when she dropped her hand. "Sexy and smart." She then continued walking.

"Wait!" He hurried to catch up, missing the feel of her hand in his. How stupid was that? "You don't know where my car is parked."

"Yes, I do." She pointed to the row where his gun-barrel black Z waited for him to push the button to unlock it. "It's that one."

"How do you know?"

In an easy movement, she spun around and walked backward. The tilt of her head indicated the same row. "You don't strike me as the Honda Civic type, and I know you'd never set foot in a Mercury Marquis unless Irma had asked you to drive her somewhere. In *her* car."

"So now I'm a stereotype?" Damn, that was even worse than being thought of as nice.

She ignored his question and strode quickly up to the car. Reverently, her hand stroked it as she walked the Z's sleek body. "It's a beauty." Her exhale came out as one loud sigh. "I'd love to own something like this, even if it made me look pretentious."

Kyle couldn't ignore the jab. "It's impractical, but not as expensive as other cars in the same class." He caught her gaze. "And it corners a hell of a lot better than a Camry or Maxima."

Mary Ann stuck her tongue out at him in response.

When he pushed the silver button, the locks clicked. He opened the passenger door and waited until Mary Ann curled into the Z.

After running around to the other side, he did the same, bending his tall frame practically in half. There was no other way of getting into it. He stretched out his legs, making sure the clutch was engaged, and pushed the START button. The engine roared to life, then settled into a gentle purr.

Mary Ann fastened her seat belt and glanced at the high-tech dashboard. "Okay, I'm convinced. This is a cool car."

"I like it," Kyle said, shifting into reverse. "It's fun to drive."

"I imagine it would be. My brother has an Audi, but it's an automatic, not a stick," Mary Ann said as he wended his way into traffic, shifting several times, climbing the gears seamlessly.

"Would you like to drive it sometime?"

She shook her head. "Can't. I've never driven a four-speed."

"It's a six-speed," he corrected defensively, as if she'd insulted his car. He remained silent until they slowed for a red light. He glanced her way. "I could teach you if you want to learn."

"You'd really let me learn on your car?"

"Yes," Kyle said.

Her pleased laughter rippled through the compact space. "I should warn you, I have five brothers. All have tried and failed to teach me the basics. Kevin, the oldest and my most patient brother, says I'm hopeless. I'm inclined to agree with him."

"Ah, another challenge." He chuckled. "And here I thought you were damn near perfect."

"Neither, not a challenge and definitely not perfect, simply giving you the facts," she said as he pulled into the parking lot of a strip mall. The café, nestled in between an auto parts store and a pool supply store, boasted wine, cheese, and pastries on the lighted storefront window.

***

Mary Ann climbed out of the car the second the locks clicked open when Kyle pressed the button to turn off the ignition.

As he joined her, she grabbed her long brown hair with one hand and flipped the strands that always seemed to get in her way over her shoulder.

"So, what do you think?" Kyle asked.

She did a full three-sixty. "Looks exactly as you described it." The wind kicked up. Forgetting all about her blowing hair, she rubbed her arms, then folded them over her chest.

"Cold?"

"A little," she said, adding silently, *or nervous.* Mary Ann couldn't believe she'd actually allowed him to kiss her after having met a scant few hours earlier. As they walked toward the shop's glass entrance, she stole a few surreptitious glances his way, trying to figure out what it was about him that had her dropping her usual cautious standards like a hot pan straight from the oven—without wearing a mitt.

Funny, but she had an idea it was because he was so nice, the exact thing he'd grumbled about. Or maybe he was more dangerous than she'd given him credit for. Either way, he was hard to resist when he flashed her that spine-tingling smile while gallantly opening the door for her.

"After you."

Restraining the urge to point out that his courtesy only corroborated her "nice" assessment, she scooted inside.

They ordered cinnamon buns and Chardonnay at Kyle's recommendation.

The waitress returned quickly with their wine. "I'll be right back with your order."

"Have you ever danced before?" she asked, picking up her glass of wine and deciding to stay on neutral ground for the moment.

His forehead furrowed and he looked at her like she'd grown a second head.

She bit back a grin. "I don't mean *dance* dance. I mean ballroom dancing."

"Oh," he said. His eyes twinkled with merriment and another shiver-producing grin took over his face. The two together were a potent weapon, strong enough, she imagined, to stop women from battling their way to the Macy's racks the day after Christmas. "No. Never."

Mary Ann eyed him over the rim of her glass. "I'm still curious as to why you agreed to take lessons with me."

"I told you—I have two left feet. Maybe lessons will help."

She didn't believe it for a minute, and the look she sent him said so.

He laughed. "Seriously? I need a reason?"

Swallowing a laugh, she nodded. "Most men I know, my brothers included, have to be half-drunk before they'll venture onto a dance floor." She gave him another pointed look. "And I'd have to hog-tie them to get them to take ballroom dancing lessons."

"I'm not most men."

"You got that right." She stopped herself from saying he was nicer than most. "Is there anyone who might object?" She should have asked earlier, like right after their kiss, but just now found the guts to do so.

"Are you asking if I have a girlfriend?"

"Yes." Maybe he was a player and kissed all the girls he met. After all, she'd pegged Steve wrong. She prayed she hadn't totally misjudged Kyle.

When he didn't say anything else, Mary Ann prodded. "Well? Is there?" She probably should let it rest, but now had to know.

Sighing, he shook his head. "No. According to certain sources, I'm not what you'd call a good catch."

She looked him up and down. "What does that mean?"

"I'm a workaholic who uses my job along with my hopeless causes to avoid intimacy. Every woman I've dated so far doesn't like that aspect of my personality."

"Hmm," she said, now studying him more critically.

Kyle held up a hand. "Stop. I'm starting to feel like an amoeba under a microscope."

Murmuring an apology, Mary Ann quickly redirected her gaze.

As she checked out the grout lines on the tile floor, he asked, "What about you?"

Surprised that he cared, she glanced at him. "Me?"

He laughed at the clueless, innocent expression she let settle on her face. "Yes, you. Any boyfriends lurking around ready to pounce?"

"Not a one. Apparently, I have too many brothers and sisters and no money."

"What?" He drew his eyebrows together. "I don't follow."

Fiddling with her hair, she glanced away. "Never mind. It was a stupid thing to say."

Their waitress interrupted their strained silence by plopping two plates on the table. Each plate held a huge glazed cinnamon bun, still warm to the touch, complete with a pat of melting butter in the center.

"So, you're in construction?" Mary Ann asked when the waitress was out of earshot. She broke off a piece of the pastry and stuck it in her mouth. After swallowing the to-die-for treat, and savoring every morsel working its way to her belly, she picked up her wine and asked before taking a sip, "What kind?"

"I build things," he said evasively, making her to want to dig deeper.

"Things?" Her eyebrows rose. "As in…?"

Kyle fingered the base of his wineglass before gripping the stem and dragging the Chardonnay to his lips for a long swallow. "My job is boring." He set the glass back on the table and ran his finger along the stem's base as he'd been doing earlier.

"Okay," she said, her gaze drawn to his hand once again. "Talking about work is off-limits." Ordinarily, that alone would have raised red flags, but the fact that he really did have capable hands lowered them somewhat. Which made no sense, other than there was something comforting in knowing a man with such strong fingers. "How about clueing me in on something that isn't?"

His smile was self-deprecating. "Sorry." He shrugged. "Surely you don't want to hear about mundane stuff like pouring concrete into steel rods and beams to create foundations?"

"When you put it like that, it does sound a little on the boring side." Her tone turned teasing as she play-slapped at him. "But I bet you have stories to tell."

"Oh, yeah?" His killer smile reached his eyes, one that could easily throw women off their train of thought. Her train had derailed back in the church parking lot. "You think I have stories to tell?"

"Absolutely!" she said. "You look like the kind of guy who's interesting." Why lie? It was the truth and she wanted to know more about him.

His grin deepened. "That's a good thing, right? What guy wouldn't want to be interesting to someone like you?" He reached for her hand and interlaced fingers, then brought both to his mouth. When his lips touched her knuckle, her eyebrows rose. "Thanks for agreeing to this impromptu date," he said in answer to her silent question.

"I thought it was just a drink and dessert. No strings attached." She gently pulled her hand out of his. Kyle's touch produced a kaleidoscope of emotions swirling inside her that she'd rather not be feeling. It was too much, too fast, and if she didn't slow things down, God only knew what could happen.

Kyle's smile died. "Sorry. That was bold of me." He shrugged. "I have no excuse, except that I feel very comfortable talking with you."

"I like you too." Bending her head and allowing her hair to partially cover her face, Mary Ann reached for her drink, hoping he hadn't seen the spark of awareness his actions had set off in her eyes. When she set the glass down, her gaze was drawn once again to his hand. "But I don't want to send any mixed signals or pretend to receive them."

"Got it." He sat up straighter. "I'm not in the market for a relationship either. I've already admitted to being a lousy catch, remember? Still, I was hoping we could at least be friends."

"Sure. Friendship works." Unfortunately, she enjoyed his company a little too much. The push-pull her turmoil generated during the last few hours kept her on edge. Allowing emotions to rule her head would be devastating. Yet, like a hungry fish spotting a worm on a hook, Mary Ann seemed drawn to the lure named Kyle Davidson.

Suddenly ballroom dancing lessons with him didn't seem like the best idea.

***

While pretending an inordinate amount of interest in his wine, Kyle let his mind spin. Mary Ann's mixed signals confused him. As did his reciprocating reaction to them, especially since he'd sworn off women after his last relationship turned ugly. The breakup with Andrea convinced him he wasn't relationship material.

Even more confusing was why Grams and Maggie were so intent on bringing them together. Mary Ann wasn't his type, if he had a type. Sure, she was attractive and he liked being with her. He damned sure liked kissing her, but he wasn't someone he'd introduce himself to, considering the defects Andrea had thrown at his feet.

Maggie knew about his long hours, as did his grandmother. Did they think that a wholesome girl like Mary Ann would change his behavior? Smiling at the thought, because so many others had tried and failed, he said, "You mentioned earlier you thought my grandmother and Maggie were in cahoots. Why?" Despite his part in this, he still felt like he was being suckered too.

"I'm not one hundred percent certain. Maggie and my mother are always trying to fix me up with someone." She shrugged. "But you're probably right. After meeting your grandmother tonight, and getting to know you, it's perfectly logical you'd spend a few hours playing bingo with a group of old ladies."

Her mischievous smile yanked on his emotional chain, sending a signal that he felt all the way to his toes. He had a hard time listening to the words flowing out of her mouth as she spoke. He dragged his gaze back up to her eyes, now alive with humor.

"Face it, Kyle." She placed her hand over his and squeezed. "You are a nice guy."

His pulse raced as he lowered his gaze to their joined hands. "There's that word again." The innocent act definitely got a rise out of him in more ways than one.

Mary Ann finally released his fingers to reach for her drink and he exhaled a relieved sigh. If she had any idea of the thoughts running through his head about what he'd like to do to her, she'd think twice before calling him a nice guy. Unfortunately, his conscience wouldn't let him go there because she was the "nice" one.

Swearing off relationships meant swearing off sex. Until he met a woman who understood him and his schedule when things got hectic, he was better off being alone. That the attitude fit in with Andrea's claim of emotional unavailability didn't bother him. His ex had wanted too much, too soon. "Think what you want, but I know the truth about my character." Thank God he'd steered Mary Ann away from the idea of a setup. "I'm glad the bingo ladies aren't part of this," he lied, adding to the ruse, just in case. "They're such romantics." Kyle grinned when Mary Ann rolled her eyes.

"What? You don't believe in love?"

"No," she said in a vehement voice, shaking her head. "Love only exists in fairy tales."

Kyle assessed her with a steady gaze. "I thought all women believed in love."

"Not this one."

His notion about love ran along a similar road. An idealist, he'd learned the hard way that love, if it existed at all, didn't last. Yet, the idea that her view was as cynical as his saddened him for some elusive reason. "You don't want kids?"

Another shake of the head was his answer, along with a quick laugh. "My mother and father have populated the world enough for three families, and I have eight brothers and sisters who are quite capable of following in their footsteps."

He shrugged. "Kids are the future." He was totally involved with his projects, which left little time for relationships, without bringing two or three rug rats of his own into the world. He sighed heavily. "We're a sad pair. Neither of us is a romantic." He picked up his wine. "I'm getting depressed." Thinking about love and kids suddenly left him feeling lonely. A totally ridiculous notion, considering his full schedule and a satisfying pet project. "I think ballroom dancing lessons will do us both a world of good."

Kyle swallowed the last of his wine as realization set in. He actually believed it.

***

Mary Ann kicked off her shoes, ran toward the bedroom, and flung herself on the bed. Cell phone in hand, she sent a quick text to Sam. If you're still up, call me! I need to talk. She glanced at the clock. Since it was 12:53, she didn't put much hope in hearing from Sam tonight. She may as well get ready for bed.

Despite being tired, she felt energized as she reached for her toothbrush. Lifting her shoulders to ease the kinks from working a full day, she rolled her head back and forth as she brushed. She rinsed her mouth, then caught her reflection in the mirror. "Don't get too excited, Mar," she warned herself mentally. Even as the warning rose up, the thought of spending the next six weeks with Kyle as a dance partner had her humming as she headed for her bedroom.

When she heard Tony Bennett's voice crooning about leaving his heart in San Francisco, Mary Ann picked up her cell phone from the dresser with a grin. She connected the call and brought the phone to her ear. "Thanks for calling!"

"Hey, Mar, what's up?" Sam asked.

Mary Ann sat on her bed cross-legged and grabbed a pillow to lean on. "I met someone tonight and I really like him."

"What's wrong with that?"

"I think he's a setup," she said, frowning. "He's too much of a gentleman to realize how devious Maggie and my mom can be."

"Ahh…" Sam said in an understanding tone. "What's his name?"

"Kyle Davidson. His grandmother's a friend of Maggie's."

"Wait, did you say Kyle Davidson?"

"Yeah," she said, nodding as if Sam could see her. "Do you know him?"

"Not personally, but I've heard James mention the name when he and Dev are together."

"James and Dev know him?" Mary Ann's stomach dropped to her feet. What did Sam's husband and Maggie's son have to do with all this? "Tell me what you know."

"Not much. He heads a small construction company that has built some of our designs around the Bay Area."

Mary Ann heaved a sigh of relief. That made sense. Both Sam and James Morrison were architects. Since moving her business across the bay not long after Sam and James got married, Mary Ann had been out of the loop. Running her own jewelry business kept her too busy for their usual weekly lunches. Nowadays, she saw Sam either on Friday nights at bingo or during a planned dinner get-together.

Mary Ann filled Sam in on her evening, including winning the dance lessons set to begin the next evening. "That's where Kyle comes in," she added. "He's agreed to go with me."

"Seems like a perfectly innocent progression of events. He sounds really nice."

Mary Ann couldn't stop from grinning. "Don't let him hear you say that. I think I've given him a complex." She glanced at the clock. "You know we've been talking for close to half an hour?"

"I called you, remember."

"Where's James? I'm sure you have better things to do than chat after midnight with me."

"As a matter of fact, he just came in. Call me after your dance class. I want to hear all about it."

"Will do." Mary Ann cut the connection and climbed into bed. As late as it was, she couldn't sleep. Kyle's smile, along with his startling green gaze, kept her tossing and turning. He'd made it clear he only wanted friendship, which was okay with her. If anything, the fact that Maggie and her mother were involved kept her from wishing for more. She could pick her own man, thank you very much. Still, she sighed and stared dreamily into the dark ceiling. Having a man like Kyle as a dancing partner excited her more than it should.

Mistake or not, she was really looking forward to ballroom dancing.

Chapter 4

Kyle disconnected the call to Holly after receiving an update on Ziggy. The kid still had an attitude, but so far seemed to realize there was no getting out of the center. Kyle then went back to pacing, practically wearing a rut in Alameda Dance Studio's hardwood floor.

When he checked his watch for the tenth time in less than fifteen minutes, he swore under his breath. He'd shown up early, his first mistake, which only compounded the rising panic he felt over the notion that Mary Ann wouldn't make it. The second had to do with looking forward to the next two hours. He shouldn't care one way or the other. Normally, he wouldn't.

The studio double doors opened, and Mary Ann glided inside as gracefully as a ballet dancer.

As she walked toward him, a grin he felt all the way to his toes snuck onto his face. "Hey, gorgeous," Kyle said when she stopped a few feet in front of him.

"Hey, gorgeous yourself." Her mouth curved into a generous smile. "I enjoyed last night."

Peering into her eyes so full of fun, he almost forgot his determination to steer clear of any involvement. Almost, but not quite. "I gather you made it home okay?"

"Yes." She held out both hands and spun around. "As you can see, I'm fine. No mishaps along the way."

He'd wanted to see her home safely, even if it meant an extra hour of driving, but Mary Ann had other ideas. She claimed to be a big girl who had taken care of herself for a long time. Kyle had had no choice but to let her go. Still, it had taken every ounce of willpower he possessed not to follow covertly behind. That alone should have sent him running in the opposite direction.

Instead, he showed up early to the studio full of anticipation, and his focus was now zeroed in on Mary Ann's smile as she mentioned something about her day that he didn't quite catch. He mentally shook off his concerns. Once his next big project began, he'd be too busy to worry about steering clear of relationships.

An older lady with military bearing clapped her hands, thankfully drawing his attention away from Mary Ann and his attraction to her.

"Hello, class. I am *Frau* Haubner," she said after everyone in the room stopped talking. "I will be your dance instructor, *ja*?" Her accent was German or Swiss, Kyle couldn't be sure, but she had that drill-sergeant demeanor down to a *T*.

"Everyone, gather around and watch. I will demonstrate the cha-cha."

Nine couples did as she'd instructed, forming a wide circle around her.

"One two, one-two-three." She repeated the cadence over and over while showing the steps. "This is the man's part," she said, making it look easy. "Now, the woman's part."

After doing so several times, she clapped her hands again. "Men, line up over there and we will try it." Her *W*s sounded like *V*s, reminding Kyle of Sister Veronica, the German-born nun who taught him in first grade who used to rap her ruler on her desk. He said as much to Mary Ann, who understood perfectly what he was talking about because her reply was a whispered, "No one dared disobey her when she gave a command, too afraid of what she might do with the ruler."

"Exactly!" He smiled. "I gather you had your own Sister issues."

"Catholic school for the first nine years." She said this like it was a badge of honor, which he could see it being, considering his few years in the parochial system. Mary Ann frowned. "High school was out of my parents' budget, so I got a reprieve and went to a public one."

"You need to listen carefully to my instructions," Frau Haubner said, staring directly at him. "Otherwise you are wasting your time—*and mine*."

Duly chastised, Kyle quickly got into line. He looked at Mary Ann, who'd turned her head, obviously laughing her ass off judging by her shaking shoulders. When she finally did glance at him with humor-filled eyes, he quickly decided he'd have to pay her back. His gaze dropped lower to her generous mouth, still smiling. The memory of kissing those amused lips emerged and desire slammed into him so fast, his head started swimming.

Whoa! His monk-like behavior was catching up with him. Deep like, his term for what he felt toward Mary Ann after one night, was hard enough to handle, but he had to nix thoughts of anything more. Wouldn't do to get involved with Grams and Maggie's fix-up. He'd never hear the end of it, once things went south.

Quit looking at her, he told himself and focused on the instructor. The sudden need gripping him was purely situational. With a little more discipline, he could keep his lustful thoughts in check.

As Kyle followed Frau Haubner's lead, he quickly picked up on the one-two, one-two-three step sequence. She observed their progress. Satisfied that the men had caught on, she turned to the women and spent several minutes taking them through the steps.

"Now we will do it together." The lady has to have sore hands, Kyle thought as more clapping rang out. "Find your partner."

Kyle watched Mary Ann start his way, wishing she weren't so wholesome and vivacious. Her cheeks, pink with exertion, and her eyes, alive with pleasure, gave her the girl-next-door look that was hard for a guy like him to resist. In his father and stepmother's crowd, most of the women were polished and their true selves were hidden deep beneath makeup and designer gowns.

Even Kyle hid his true identity, but for a different reason. He didn't like admitting to being the Davidson behind Davidson Construction because people always treated him differently afterward, especially women. He doubted someone as grounded as Mary Ann would, but why take the chance?

The door to the dance studio opened and Frau Haubner stopped in midsentence to stare down the couple who'd just stepped inside. "You are late." Her voice rose as she added, "I will accept your tardiness tonight. For future reference, if you can't make it to my class on time, do not bother to come at all."

If she'd had a ruler, Kyle was sure she'd rap the guy's knuckles. He was about to crack a joke about it, but when he turned to Mary Ann, her face had gone white and her smile, now frozen, no longer held the earlier warmth. Her attention was glued to the new arrivals. He glanced at them, then back at her. "You know them?"

"You could say that," Mary Ann said, shrugging and focusing on the oak planks beneath their feet. "Forget about them." She grabbed his arm and he reached his other hand at her waist to get into the dance hold.

Frau Haubner's no-nonsense command had the late arrivals joining in, and Kyle had no more time to worry about Mary Ann's weird response to the couple. It took all of his concentration just to keep up with the dragon lady's directives. He hadn't lied about his two left feet, but he had to give the woman credit. After practicing the other steps she'd shown the class in the last twenty minutes, he could actually lead an easy cha-cha. It was Mary Ann who kept missing steps.

The music trailed off and Kyle signaled for her to do one last turn. As before, she ended up stepping on his foot.

"I'm sorry. I can't seem to get the steps down."

"You're doing fine." Even as he spoke the platitude, he sensed her distraction had something to do with the two latecomers.

"Take five," Frau Haubner said, adding another clap.

Kyle walked with Mary Ann to the corner where they'd left their jackets and other possessions earlier. He reached for her water bottle, handed it to her, then reached for his own and uncapped the lid. "Is everything all right?"

Mary Ann downed several mouthfuls, then wiped her mouth with the back of her hand. "Yes." She set the bottle down and picked up the hand towel to wipe more sweat off her neck and brow. "I'm just a little overwhelmed." A wry smile tugged at her lips. "It looks so easy on *Dancing with the Stars*."

"Oh, I don't know. I'm catching on quick enough."

"You're a ringer." Her eyebrows rose as she brought the bottle to her mouth. "You told me you had two left feet."

He shrugged. "Hidden talents?"

Her short laugh zinged through his ear and landed in his gut. He shook the sensation and narrowed his gaze. "You seem distracted," he said when he caught her casting another brief at the couple in question. "What's with them?"

Her gaze avoided his as she took another sip. "I don't know what you mean."

Not about to let it go, he said, "I mean, since the moment they've arrived, you've clammed up. You're definitely not the same woman I played bingo with last night."

A loud sigh was her only answer as she paid an inordinate amount of attention to the few drops from condensation on her water bottle. She fingered one of the drops and followed it down the length of the bottle before glancing back at him.

He lifted an eyebrow. "Well? Are you going to tell me?"

"Mary Ann?"

Kyle glanced in the direction of the voice, as the male half of the very couple they were discussing said, "I thought that was you."

Mary Ann tensed. Even her hair looked stiff. From his vantage point, her smile appeared pasted on, like she was gritting her teeth to keep her lips curved.

"Hello, Steve." Straight as a board, she brushed a strand of hair behind her ear. "What a surprise."

"I can't believe we've bumped into each other twice in two days, when we haven't seen each other in almost two years."

"Guess we're lucky." Mary Ann showed more teeth, but the frost in her expression hadn't melted.

Oblivious to her facial cue, Steve turned to Kyle and stuck out his hand. "I'm Steve Henderson and this is my wife, Taylor." He reached behind him and Kyle finally noticed the woman.

"Hey, Steve. Taylor." Kyle shook both hands. "I'm Kyle Davidson."

"So are you two dating?" Taylor asked, looking down her nose at Mary Ann, her eyes full of disdain.

Kyle interrupted Mary Ann's answer to wrap an arm around her waist. "As a matter of fact, we are," he lied, not completely sure why he was doing so, but positive it was the right thing to do. When Mary Ann looked at him, her eyes wide with question, he smiled. "Isn't that right?"

The gratitude swelling in her warm smile threw him completely off balance and he couldn't stop a generous grin from taking over the lower half of his face.

They had no more time for conversation because clapping filled the air. "God, that woman should get a ruler and tap it," he said. The sharp sound Frau Haubner made by putting her hands together grated on his nerves. Kyle turned to Steve and Taylor. "Nice meeting you," he said, praying they'd get the hint and leave. By the way they treated Mary Ann, they clearly didn't see her as a friend. And it was obvious Mary Ann didn't like them. The best solution was to steer clear of them.

The next hour wasn't as much fun as the first hour, mainly because Kyle was now aware of the undercurrents between the Hendersons and Mary Ann. Glancing at the couple who appeared like they'd stepped out of a magazine, Kyle swore under his breath. They were too much like his father and his stepmother. And Kyle had long ago decided he'd never be like them.

"Listen up, class!" Thankfully, the demand came out clap-free and everyone in the studio quieted and glanced toward Frau Haubner. "We will be learning three dances during the next five lessons. You should all practice your cha-cha during the week. It's one of the easiest dances, so we will review it at our next class and move on to the waltz. During our last class, we will have a little dance competition, *ja?*" She grinned and her granite expression softened a bit. She almost looked pretty. "The winner will receive another six dance lessons."

Kyle guided Mary Ann to their belongings in the corner. "We're going to win the competition," he said, turning to her, letting her see the determination in his eyes.

She laughed. "Don't be silly. We don't need to win." Their gazes met, and her eyes filled with moisture. She grabbed his hand and squeezed. "You've done more than you know. I can't thank you enough." Her attention wandered to across the room and Kyle glanced in the same direction.

Steve was helping his wife into her expensive fur-lined leather jacket.

"Don't mention it." He ran a hand through his hair, then glanced back at Mary Ann. "I'd really like an explanation as to why it was necessary."

"We dated long enough for me to realize he cares more about money and what people with it think of him." Mary Ann slung her bag over her shoulder and started for the door.

Kyle stood staring at the empty space in stunned silence. Finally, he hurried to catch up. "Wait! We have to set up a time to practice." Being alone together might strain his resolve, but there was no way he was going to let Steve and Taylor win. Especially after what she'd just revealed.

People with the advantages of money, namely those like the Hendersons and his stepmother, had no idea what it was like to struggle. Despite having been born with a silver spoon, Kyle knew. He'd worked damned hard only to be caught up in the construction downturn and watch his business slide into the red. His father had bailed him out—something Kyle had hated, but had allowed. Going under would have taken too many hardworking people down at the same time. Unlike his peers, Kyle cared about what happened to those not as lucky as him.

Chapter 5

The bell over the door tinkled as Kyle entered Good Eats Café. His thoughts were on Grams and her manipulations, so he almost bumped into a man on his way out. "Excuse me," he said, holding the door open. The guy murmured a thank-you and scooted out. Kyle let go of the door and walked up to the counter, still wondering about how she'd done it. A bitter pill to swallow for sure, made even more bitter if she found out they'd spent two hours together after bingo and were planning on practicing together.

"Can I help you?" said a perky teen with braces behind the counter when it was Kyle's turn.

Weekday mornings the place was as busy as it was in the evenings. The tables were full of people plugging into the Internet while enjoying an early morning treat and coffee. And the line still reached almost to the door for those, like him, who ordered their coffee and sweets to go.

Kyle pointed to the cheese Danish his grandmother loved. "One of those and I'll also take a hot cinnamon bun with melted butter." His favorite. He handed the girl his Good Eats card along with a five dollar bill.

"You have a free pastry on your card for your next visit," she said, grinning with a face full of metal and handing him change.

"Thanks." He grabbed the sack of breakfast goodies and holding on to his laptop, he pushed his way out the door. The trip to Grams's house took less than five minutes.

"Grams?" he yelled after letting himself in with his key. "I come bearing sweet gifts."

He caught sight of her walking down the stairs at a pace that belied her eighty years. "You're looking spry this morning." The stroke she'd had two years ago hadn't affected her energy level, thank God. He bent to give her a kiss.

"I wish I felt as spry as I look." After graduating from physical therapy, Grams kept in shape by taking yoga and Zumba classes, along with weight training several times a week at her local gym. She glanced at the bag in his hand and grinned. "I have the coffee ready."

"Next one is free." He held up his card.

"That's my boy," she said, patting his cheek.

His cheapness was a running joke among those who knew him well. Kyle preferred to think of himself as frugal. Grams was the only person he knew who was cheaper than him. After all, she'd lived through the Great Depression and had taught him that to waste was to want. She abhorred what she called "our throwaway society."

The scent of freshly brewed coffee filled the air. Kyle smiled and followed her through the hallway toward her cozy kitchen.

At the doorway she glanced over her shoulder. "What did you think of Mary Ann?"

Sighing, he shook his head, watching her move farther into the room.

"Please don't tell me the dance lessons were part of some fiendish plan," he said as she filled two mugs with coffee.

"Okay, I won't," she said, handing him one of the mugs. She reached for hers and took a sip. "Ah, hot and strong, exactly the way I like it." A smug smile settled over her face as she nodded to the bag in his other hand. "Well, are you going to stand there worrying about the shenanigans of a bunch of old ladies, or are you going to eat?"

An unsettling sensation traveled up his spine as he sat and unwrapped the bag, pulling out her plastic container and popping off the lid. He set the Danish in front of her, then reached for his cinnamon bun.

They ate in silence, but the entire time Kyle's mind spun, searching for a way to get Grams to open up about what she and Maggie were up to.

It was bad enough to get roped into this, yet he felt that if Mary Ann ever found out, she'd be mad as hell. By association, he'd be in the direct line of fire of the fallout. After getting to know her a little better, that was the last thing he wanted.

"So, do you like her?"

He shrugged noncommittally. God only knew what she'd do if she knew he liked her more than a little bit.

"What kind of answer is that?"

"It doesn't matter whether I like her or not, Grams. I'm

emotionally unavailable, as Andrea put it."

"Andrea was always too demanding and had a tendency to be overdramatic at times. I'm not surprised she blamed you."

"What if she's right?"

"Fiddlesticks." She scowled. "You simply haven't met the right woman yet."

He scowled back, letting her know that trick didn't work on him. "You're not trying to set us up? Because if you are, I don't—"

"No! I would never do such a thing," she said, placing a hand over her heart, a shocked expression filling her features. Grams then grabbed his hand and squeezed. "She's had a string of bad luck lately with men, and Maggie thought if someone like you showed interest, it would help her to get back on the horse, so to speak. You're such a wonderful grandson. I know you'd never take advantage of her vulnerability."

Eyeing her, Kyle absorbed the meaning of her admission. Great. Now he was stuck in the middle. He finally sighed. "Don't worry. I wouldn't think of hurting her, but let's drop the subject."

Grams took a sip of coffee and bit into her Danish, obviously reflecting as she chewed. "All right, I will, but Maggie's not going to like hearing that all her planning has gone to pot."

His smile was quick. "You can tell Maggie that overwatering and too much fertilizer aren't helping." Damn if these women weren't tenacious in their matchmaking. "If I did happen to find Mary Ann interesting, your actions only push me in the opposite direction." He set his mug on the table and caught her gaze. "Both of you should sit back and let nature take its course," he said, tossing her a bone to chew on.

When her gleeful cackle rose up, he stiffened. He probably shouldn't have given her false hope. Unfortunately, without doing so, he'd have to sit through more of her arm-twisting.

"Consider the subject dropped, but I retain the right to ask how the dance lessons are going every now and again."

Amused, he nodded. "I can live with that."

"Good. Now, let's talk about your father."

As quickly as he'd relaxed, his back went ramrod. "I'd rather not."

"He's stopping by on his way to the office." She glanced at the kitchen clock. "I expect him any moment."

Feeling put on the spot as well as a little betrayed, he scrutinized her face. "I wish you'd told me ahead of time."

"Why? He's your father."

"You know why."

"Surely you can have a cup of coffee with him? He is trying."

Kyle grunted begrudgingly. After all, his dad did save his company by buying him out and leaving him in charge. Even though they now worked in the same building, Kyle rarely saw him. "It's a little too late to start acting like a father, don't you think?"

The wounded look that crossed her features stopped him cold, and he glanced at the table feeling like he'd just kicked a puppy.

"He's your father, for heaven's sake," she said in an exasperated tone.

Kyle bit back a nasty response and sighed. "A cup of coffee won't hurt," he murmured, knowing it would please her. Besides, when Grams got something in her head, she was as stubborn as him. That was probably why they understood each other so well. "I'll be extra nice for your sake, but that's all I can promise."

"That's a start." Her satisfied grin was back and he wondered why he let her manipulate him. Yet as soon as the thought was out, he knew the reason. He loved her and he'd go far to make her last years on earth easier than the years she'd spent raising him.

The doorbell chimed, interrupting her next sentence. She rose and headed toward the hallway, saying over her shoulder, "Speak of the devil."

Yeah, Ronald Davidson was the devil, all right. Kyle lifted the mug to his mouth and sipped, wishing the memories of the past would allow him to forgive and forget like his grandmother expected. Some things couldn't be forgiven with an "I'm sorry."

"It's good to see you, son."

Kyle looked up to see his dad at the kitchen doorway, and quickly stood. "Good to see you too." He held out his hand when his father moved close enough, but instead of shaking it, Ronald pulled him into a bear hug.

Caught off guard, Kyle returned the hug, stunned that emotion welled in the back of his throat. "You're looking good, Dad," he said when he could speak without sounding sappy. His father had a few more wrinkles and his temples were completely gray, but he still had the posture of a man who was used to taking charge.

"Would you like a cup of coffee, Ron?" Grams asked, holding up the pot.

"Thanks, Mom." He nodded. "I'd love one."

Kyle ran a hand through his hair. "If I'd have known you were coming, I'd have brought you something too," he said, the tip of his head indicating the pastries on the table.

His father offered a wry smile. "We both know that's a blatant lie. If you'd known about my dropping by this morning, you'd have skipped the visit altogether."

Flabbergasted that his dad had nailed it correctly, Kyle cleared his throat, unable to think of a suitable comeback. They hadn't seen each other in weeks. If only the memory of his mother's pained expression would fade, he might be able to dig out the anger toward the man buried deep inside his soul and get rid of it once and for all.

Yet the image wouldn't die, even after almost two decades. Despite being only ten years old when his mother and father had their last fight, he could still hear the shouts. Ronald had told her to get out and never come back. She'd said she never would. And she never did.

Amelia Davidson had died in a car accident the same night, leaving Kyle with a dad who submerged himself in work while forgetting he had a son to raise.

Kyle glanced at the older man, seeing a look of yearning in his expression, the same one that made him feel guilty for his inability to give what his father seemed to need. Some sort of connection that wouldn't come. Kyle would love nothing more than to forget and forgive. Even if he could forgive Ronald Davidson for virtually kicking his mom out, he couldn't get past the fact that his dad wasn't there when Kyle had needed him most. How did one go about manufacturing something never developed in the first place? Ronald was an absentee parent who left the hard part to his own mother and then expected Kyle to pretend it had never happened.

Kyle loved his dad. Always did and always would, but he'd learned early on to guard his heart against the hurt of rejection. Too bad his dad hadn't loved him enough not to pawn him off on Grams in order to focus on his new wife and child.

"How's Stephanie?" Kyle asked, pushing the idea of his father still needing him out of his mind. Ronald was doing a much better job with his second family.

"She's still volunteering like crazy." He fingered his tie, then twisted his neck as if to get comfortable. "Brad has a lead part in *Oliver*, his eighth-grade play. He's hoping you'll come." Ronald sighed. "And so am I."

"Won't my presence put a crimp in Stephie's plans?" His

stepmother had never liked him. True, he hadn't liked her at first glance when he'd told her she could never take his mother's place. From there, things had gone south. Kyle shared the blame equally, but how else could he react?

As far as Kyle was concerned, his father had made his choice long ago.

"I'll be there," Grams said. "I got a new camera, but I can't figure it out, so I was hoping you'd go to take pictures for me." Grams lifted one brow, her questioning gaze zeroed in on him.

Kyle glanced from his grandmother's expectant face to his dad's. "Of course I'll be there too," he said, relenting. The only innocent one in this was his half brother. Now that Bradley was older, Kyle had made more of an effort to stay in touch with the kid. The Internet was great for that, as was texting.

Ronald smiled. "He'll be glad to see you. He's always talking about you."

"How'd he do on his history exam?"

"Got an A." His father's expression softened. "Thanks for helping him."

He shrugged. "That's what big brothers are for. Helping." Hell, if he could help others not even related to him with his kids camp, the least he could do was help his own flesh and blood. Kyle didn't add his true thoughts on the subject, because to do so might put a monkey wrench in the communication wheels that had begun to turn between them. At least Ziggy was doing better.

They discussed the play and his brother for a few minutes before Ronald cleared his throat and added, "Maybe the three of us can go to a football game or something. Or maybe hockey?"

"That'd be great, Dad." Kyle's smile reached his eyes. "Maybe I could take a couple of my kids from the camp." The camp for underprivileged children was his pet project and every child who lived there was special. It was also a bone of contention between him and his father.

His father put up a hand. "Now, son, you know how Stephie is about having those kids around Brad." His exhale was one huge sigh. "Raising kids is hard enough without exposing them to bad influences."

"They're just kids. Too many start becoming bad influences because of thinking like that." Kyle shook his head as disappointment swallowed him whole. Nothing had really changed. Ronald thought it foolish for Kyle to spend his mother's inheritance on society's problem children, especially since he wasn't related to them.

When Kyle caught another one of his grandmother's pleading stares, he gave a resigned sigh. His dad was trying to open up and act like he gave a damn. It wouldn't hurt to spend a couple of hours with them. "Name the date and I'll be there. I know Brad would really like it." He'd take his kids another time.

"You'll have to stop by for pictures before you go. I want to have all my boys together in one room." The smile on Grams's face made Kyle realize how little it took to make her happy.

She'd also become an expert at defusing tension when the conversation lagged as it did many times in the last half hour.

Kyle glanced at his watch and finally stood. "I've got an appointment in twenty minutes, and if I don't leave now, I'll never make it."

This time he took the initiative and hugged his dad, who'd also stood. "It was nice seeing you, Dad."

"You too, son. Brad's play is next Friday. I'll call you with specifics," Ronald added as Kyle let go of him and turned to his grandmother.

She looked up at him with gratitude, a look that had him wishing he could let go of the anger. Kyle was tired of holding on to it so tightly. He simply didn't know how to let it go.

"I'll give you a call later to let you know how my next dance class with Mary Ann goes," he offered instead. "That way you'll have something to tell Maggie." He wasn't about to tell her that he had plans to take her to dinner tonight after the class. That would only add fuel to her matchmaking fire.

***

Irma kissed Kyle. "Drive carefully." Her grandson was special, like a second son to her.

He hugged her, then leaned back and grinned. "I always drive carefully."

"Ha! I bet you have a hard time keeping within the speed limit." She caught his amused gaze and winked. "I know if that Z were mine, I'd be using the brake more than a little bit."

Ronald laughed and Kyle joined in. "That's why you'll never drive my car."

Irma tsk-tsked. "I guess I'll have to settle for a boring ol' Volvo."

"If you play your cards right, I'll give you a ride," he said with a wink.

"You will?" Surprised, Irma squelched a pleased cackle. Kyle was such a joy.

"Sure." His grin matched hers. "And you know I always follow the rules." Seconds later he was gone.

"The ones you can't bend," Irma whispered to his departing back. She closed the front door and turned to look at her son. Holding his gaze, she said in a louder voice, "I wish you'd tell him the truth about his mother. He has a right to know."

Without answering, Ronald swiped a hand over his face and rubbed the back of his neck. Finally, he sighed. "My reasons for remaining silent haven't changed, and even if they had, it's too late for honesty."

"You underestimate him. You always have." She headed for the kitchen. "He's been mature enough to deal with the truth for quite some time now."

Ronald followed her into the room and as he leaned against the counter, she asked, "Would you like another cup of coffee?"

"Yes, please." He glanced at her. "I hate the idea of shattering his illusions of Amelia."

"Which means you can keep the wall you created up so you don't have to get close to him."

"Is that how you see it?"

"Yes. I think it's past time one of you stopped being so pigheaded. It's damn well past time for you to stop fearing his rejection and realize life is short. You can't get back what you've already squandered."

"After twenty years, I'm in too deep." A self-deprecating smile crossed Ronald's face. "He'll probably hate me all the more for keeping her illness a secret."

Irma folded her arms to keep from shaking some sense into him. "This is something that should come from you. If he finds out from another source, you run the risk of losing him forever."

Ronald frowned and his expression darkened. "Let me think about it."

Chapter 6

Kyle parked a block from Mary Ann's apartment, then unfolded himself from the car and headed toward her street at a fast pace. When he turned the corner, two panhandlers were flashing their OUT OF WORK - PLEASE HELP signs a few feet in front of him. Kyle stopped and reached for two business cards from inside his pocket.

He wrote his foreman's name and number on the back of each. Holding them out, he said, "If you're serious about working, give this guy a call."

One of the men looked at him like he'd lost his marbles. The other's eyes perked up in interest. Kyle whipped out his billfold and handed that guy a twenty. "Get a decent meal, and you can buy some jeans and a shirt at the Goodwill not too far from here before you go."

The homeless man stared in wonder at the money in his hand. "I don't know what to say," he stammered.

"You don't have to say anything. Show up and help yourself. If you work, you'll be paid. If you work hard, you'll earn yourself a steady job." It was always easier to spot kids who'd benefit from a leg up, but adults took a little more finessing.

"Thanks, man. You're a lifesaver." As he started off in the direction Kyle had indicated, the other guy threw out some attitude with his chest. "Where's my twenty?" he asked in a menacing voice.

Some, like the man in his face, only wanted a handout. All that did was make their problems worse, in Kyle's opinion. "Sorry. I can't help you there, but if you're looking to work to earn some, I'm sure my foreman could use an extra hand."

"I don't want no goddamned job. I want money."

He shook his head and turned to go, but the guy's hand on his arm stopped him. "Don't turn your back on me, buddy."

As fast as a striking snake, Kyle grabbed the hand that was on his arm and spun the guy around, twisting his arm in a hold behind his back. "I gave you my answer. I'd be glad to help you with a job like your sign says. Since you aren't interested, I can only assume you don't need it and hence you don't need my money."

When Kyle loosened his grip, the man yanked his hand away. Rubbing his wrist, he gave Kyle another dirty look before stomping off in the other direction, calling Kyle all kinds of ugly names under his breath.

Sighing, Kyle stuck the card the guy hadn't wanted back in his pocket. Fred, his foreman, was always looking for able-bodied men who'd show up every day, ready to work, the key word being work. The construction business was very fluid. Good employees were hard to find. It amazed Kyle that in this day and age too many wanted a free ride or wanted to start at the top, rather than the bottom. Neither Kyle nor Fred was willing to teach them what their parents should have. Kyle had enough to handle helping kids without advantages become adults who contributed to society, rather than took away from it.

Halfway down the next block, Kyle found Mary Ann's apartment building. He rang the buzzer.

"Is that you, Kyle?"

"Expecting anyone else?"

A quick laugh was his answer as the door clicked open. "Up the stairs one flight. Turn right. Third door on the left."

Kyle easily found his way to her door, which was open an inch. He knocked and it swung in all the way.

Mary Ann greeted him with a warm smile. She had on old jeans and an oversized sweatshirt that covered her lush figure and made her appear small and dainty. After having been stepped on so many times during their dance lesson, he knew for a fact those tiny feet packed a wallop. Still, her cheeks were rosy and her eyes sparkled with mischief, and Kyle got caught up in that hazel gaze.

Unable to resist giving her a wide grin, he asked, "Ready to practice?"

"Of course."

Another laugh brought his gaze to her full lips. He didn't like admitting to himself that he still thought a lot about the night in the church parking lot when he'd kissed her. Did she ever think about it? His focus roamed higher. When their eyes reconnected, he caught a spark of awareness.

Mary Ann lowered her gaze as her hair fell forward to cover her face. "Come on in." The move wasn't fast enough to hide the pink of her cheeks, now turning a couple of shades darker. "I moved my furniture against the walls so we'd have some room." She stepped aside and waited to close the door until he was well into the room. Without looking at him, she led him toward the sofa.

"Would you like a drink?"

As usual, her hair was down, but was full of curls that looked softer. If he was curious as to the texture before, now his curiosity grew. His fingers itched to run freely through her thick dark mane. It was shinier tonight. He glanced at the recessed lights on the ceiling and decided lighting had to be the reason. Still, he had to subdue an urge to touch one of the curls that bounced behind her as he followed Mary Ann toward her kitchen area.

The studio apartment wasn't big. Her furnishings said a lot about her, down-to-earth but with quirky and unexpected surprises like a troll doll, similar to the ones he'd seen last Friday during bingo, and a couple of Mardi Gras beaded necklaces. "Have you been to New Orleans?" he asked, seeing the beads hanging on a light sconce.

"No. But it's on my bucket list. I got those at a party for my limbo."

"Oh?" He eyed her with more interest. "You can limbo?"

"Yep. I can go real low." Opening her fridge and looking inside it, she said, as if changing the subject, "I have a couple of Paulaners."

Kyle took the hint and decided to humor her. For now. "My favorite imported beer."

"Really? Seems we have something in common." Mary Ann uncapped one bottle, then the second, and handed it to him.

"Thanks." He took a sip, washing the last of the taste of the panhandler out of his mind. He would always offer help, but sometimes it took more than his desire to do the right thing. The individual had to do his part. That was why Kyle was so insistent on helping needy kids. He didn't want any who went through his camp to be like the guy on the street, or worse, end up dead or in jail because of drug addiction or alcoholism. He'd spoken to Holly that morning and her positive report on Ziggy had made it all worthwhile. Kyle knew the kid would come around eventually, especially when given a better option.

"Dinner is on me. It's the least I can do for making you practice," he said, following Mary Ann back into her dining area.

She pulled out a chair and sat. After taking a long sip, she set the beer aside and placed her elbows on the table. "I've decided we may have a small chance at winning." Her expression skeptical, she rested her chin on her intertwined fingers and glanced at him from across the table.

Kyle brought the bottle to his mouth for another sip, then studied her face over the top. "You don't think we can pull it off?" Mary Ann shrugged. "I scoped out the competition and one or two of those couples are really good."

"That's okay." Kyle's smile was quick. "I'm not worried about them, but I sure as hell am going to out dance your friends."

A grimace took over her face. "I've already told you, they aren't my friends."

"He thinks so, but that seems to be a bone of contention for his wife."

"I don't know why she would hate me, other than she's a snob," Mary Ann said, shaking her head. "She doesn't even know me."

"What about him?" Kyle was more than curious. "I notice he hasn't gotten the message that you two aren't friends."

Mary Ann paid an inordinate amount of attention to her beer, then eventually lifted it to her lips and said before taking a drink, "God only knows what makes Steve Henderson tick. I don't know why I ever thought he'd be husband material."

"Husband material?" The comment shouldn't have surprised him, but it did. She seemed too smart to fall for a guy like Henderson.

"Yeah." A wry expression slid over her face and she frowned. "I thought we might end up married, but when the time came to propose, he broke up with me instead. Said he needed some time to think about what he wanted."

"Ouch."

She laughed, but it sounded too brittle to be real. "Three months later he married Taylor. They now have six-month-old triplets."

"Double ouch." His gaze narrowed. "So this was fairly recent?"

"Eighteen months, one week, and five days," she said, then snorted. "But who's counting?"

"Wow." Kyle could only stare at her. "He must have meant something to you if you're counting the days."

"No. As a matter of fact, it's just the opposite. I use the date as a reminder to never get involved with the wrong guy again."

"Hmmm. I hear you," he said, thinking of his own failed relationships. "I've sworn off relationships for the time being. I can't seem to find a balance."

"We're getting off track." Mary Ann jumped up. She came around the table, reached for his hand, and pulled him up. "Let's get this practice going. I taped last week's *DWTS*." She led him to the sofa.

"What's *DWTS*?" he asked, getting comfortable.

"*Dancing with the Stars*." She grabbed the remote off the coffee table. "Tony and Katrina are both doing cha-chas with their partners." She clicked the remote and the TV came alive with dancers.

Kyle watched, too stunned to miss a moment as the sinking sensation in his gut dropped lower. When the music died and the two dancers moved across to get the judges' comments, Kyle glanced at Mary Ann. "They are really good." His gaze took in his two left feet. Even though he'd made a pretty decent showing last Friday night, he was nowhere near the level of the two novices on the screen.

"I memorized a couple of the dance steps." She waited until he glanced her way. "Want to see?"

He swallowed hard. "Yeah."

She did several maneuvers that looked too intricate for him to ever grasp. When he moved to shake his head, she pulled him to his feet. "Try it. One two, one two three. One two, cha cha cha." She did the steps a couple more times. "Watch my feet." Kyle looked down as she added, "I figured out what Tony does and what she does."

After several minutes of watching, Kyle followed her steps, feeling like a duck out of water. When he practically fell on his butt, he put up a hand. "I don't think—"

She cut him off. "I couldn't do it either my first time, but I kept doing it over and over until it became second nature." Determination was etched into her expression. "Now try it again and do it until you get the steps down."

"Slave driver," he said under his breath. For the next twenty minutes, he did nothing but the pattern she'd shown him. At first he couldn't get through it without messing up. Several times. But finally, the steps started to click.

He did the full routine without a mistake and she clapped. "Okay, now we'll do it to music to see how it feels."

When she turned on the CD player and the song started playing, they stepped into hold. He got the count in his head and together they danced the steps a dozen or so times. She broke hold and wrapped him in a bear hug. "You did it! See, you can dance when you put your mind to it."

"What's next," he asked, trying to ignore the spicy scent she wore. Like pine needles and lavender. He decided it was best not to meet her gaze, so he nodded, grinning like an idiot.

"Watch and learn."

They went through half a dozen patterns and together they came up with ninety seconds of cha-cha. After practicing those steps, Kyle suddenly understood why Frau Haubner was so fond of clapping. It had something to do with ballroom dancing.

The music died and he glanced at Mary Ann. "I wonder what she'll say when we do this cha-cha?"

"She'll have to realize we did practice."

"Let's try it once more, adding the turn we learned in class." She quickly agreed and reset the music. They got into hold and when the notes were right, Kyle signaled Mary Ann to begin. Now that his feet knew what to do, he had the freedom to surreptitiously watch her wiggle those sexy hips. And the way she snapped those feet to the beat made it hard to concentrate on anything else but the sway of her body. Thank God for his photographic memory. Otherwise, he'd be the one stepping on a few toes this time.

His gaze found hers. That saucy smile she flashed worked for the dance and him. Hell, he'd follow her anywhere. Instead, he tried to concentrate more on leading.

Gazes still connected, they finished.

The second he dropped his hands, she threw her arms around him. "We're going to win. I just know it."

Warmth filtered up Kyle's midsection toward his neck as his body responded to her closeness. This time it wasn't just her spicy scent that assaulted his senses. His groin responded when her knees brushed his, and her breasts pressed against his chest. It was pure torture to hold perfectly still and pretend he felt nothing.

When she let go and glanced expectantly at him, he felt another jolt through his system. Unwilling to let her see his reaction, he grabbed his jacket. "I think it's time we thought about food. I'm famished." For more than food, he thought, and if he stayed here he might do or say something he couldn't take back. "Do you have a favorite place?"

"I love Italian." With purse in hand, Mary Ann opened a closet door and extracted a jacket.

When he held out his hand, she looked at him funny. "Your jacket," he said, indicating the navy coat she held in her hand.

"Oh, yeah." Again that darker pink hit her cheeks. On her, the color only added to her beauty. She had the face of a model but her body was too lush, to his good fortune or misfortune. Most models he'd come across had been skin and bones, no shape whatsoever. He liked a bit of meat on women. He liked curves most of all, and Mary Ann had a curvaceous body to tempt even Saint Peter himself.

Once outside, Kyle was thankful of the dark that hid his thoughts. As they walked, he was also thankful they were side by side. That way Mary Ann couldn't see into his eyes to read the thoughts he had a difficult time hiding. He found her more than attractive on every level. She was funny, smart, and driven. Those characteristics, along with her body and looks, did strange things to his insides. He'd never known anyone like her.

Of course, she was a little standoffish about relationships. But then, so was he. Maybe if they went about it slowly, things would work out better than they had with Andrea. The memory of his last date with the woman came to mind and he sighed. He'd made her totally unhappy. She seemed to change over the course of the year they'd dated, going from a fun-loving, free-spirited girl to a clingy, questioning, overdemanding woman. She didn't like the fact that he spent so much time with his kids. Plus, when he wasn't with his kids he was working. She'd claimed that once he had her, he ignored her. Funny, but Kyle didn't think he'd ever ignored her, but…well, it had to be true because Andrea's metamorphosis was all the proof he needed for him to realize he wasn't relationship material. He didn't want to admit that he might share similarities with his dad.

"So, tell me something about your childhood," Kyle asked when the waitress was out of earshot after taking their orders.

"Like what?" Looking very relaxed, Mary Ann leaned her chin on her intertwined fingers.

Kyle lifted a shoulder in a half shrug. "Anything you want to share."

"Anything?"

"Yes, and the juicier the better, as Maggie would say." He looked pointedly at her. "After all, we need to break the ice and get to know each other."

"Hmmm." Mary Ann averted her gaze, slowly shaking her head.

50

"That's a hard question to answer because I'm not sure I want you to know any of my secrets."

"You have secrets?" A smile lurked at the corners of his mouth. "Even better."

Grinning, Mary Ann play-slapped at his shoulder, then her expression turned serious. "Let me think." She studied the table in front of her for so long, Kyle was about to say something when she looked up. "I took the heat for my brother when he let the frog out of our older brother's tank. Poor Croaker ended up smothered in cat hair under the dresser, at which point he really had croaked." She offered a rueful smile. "I had to sit in the corner for a long time for that one and had to buy him a new frog, which is why I remember it so well. Took me six weeks to pay for it. I was five at the time. To this day, everyone thinks I did it. They also think I have a mean streak because of it."

"They obviously don't know you."

"Oh, don't worry," she quickly interjected. "I've done my fair share of things to earn the title. When you have a ton of brothers and sisters, you have to develop defense mechanisms as well as a thick skin because someone is always at their worst."

"I didn't have any siblings growing up, but I can empathize with the mean streak."

"You?" The look she threw his way said *no way.* "Not the proverbial nice guy."

He laughed. "You wouldn't say that if you knew my true nature."

"So now we're getting to the nitty-gritty," she said, and gave him a hand gesture that said, *Come on, out with it.*

Kyle straightened in the booth. "I'm not so sure I want to be knocked off my pedestal."

Her eyebrow lifted and every cell in her body urged him to confess.

"Don't say I never tried to warn you." He cleared his throat. "When I was twelve, I put itching powder in my stepmother's lingerie drawer."

"That's horrible." She put a hand to her mouth, as if to hide a smile.

He shrugged. "Of course it was." He didn't add that it was one of the nicer stunts he'd pulled trying to gain his father's attention. "As an adult looking back, I cringe at the thought that I could be so cruel. Obviously, I craved attention." All kids did. Kyle had learned the hard way that if a kid didn't get it by being good, being bad worked just as well.

"Did you get it?"

"Yes, but not as I'd hoped." Unfortunately, acting out negatively had only hurt himself and never really solved the problem. "I got sent to live with my grandmother. The itching powder incident was the last straw, according to my stepmother. She essentially made my father choose. Me or her." He picked up his water glass as he lifted his shoulders. "I lost."

Mary Ann's amusement died. "That's even more horrible," she said, her jaw dropping a good inch.

"I thought so too." Kyle shrugged again. "I still dislike her, but I've learned to tolerate her. She's my brother's mother, after all. He's a great kid." It surprised him that Brad was turning out so well-adjusted, considering his parents. Kyle glanced at Mary Ann's face, where a wealth of sympathy resided. "Don't."

"Don't what?" Her features now held curiosity, but the sympathy still lurked in those expressive eyes.

"Go thinking you can make up for what I lost in childhood."

"I wasn't thinking that," she said almost too quickly. She toyed with her empty water glass. "In fact, I was thinking how lucky I am to have my big family. Hearing you talk about your childhood made me realize how much I have to be thankful for. My parents love all of their kids equally, but they adjust for different needs."

The waitress arrived with their meal, a timely interruption. For the rest of the meal Kyle kept the conversation flowing, at the same time carefully avoiding the earlier topic. Thinking about his childhood depressed him.

Finally, he signed the charge slip and stood. "Let's get out of here."

Outside, Kyle breathed in the crisp fall air. It was misting, and the moisture felt cool on his face as he lifted it up while walking side by side with Mary Ann.

They'd walked to the restaurant earlier. As they retraced their steps, cars honked and dogs barked, yet the silence between them felt natural rather than stifling, like they'd done this same thing a hundred times before.

"I love nights like this," he finally said as they neared her apartment building. The street noise had lessened. "The fog rolling in, the foghorns in the background wailing, and everything else is still."

"Yeah, I know what you mean." She shivered.

He stopped to look at her, then smiled. Her teeth were chattering and she had her hands in her pockets. "Cold?"

She shrugged. "A little."

Kyle didn't need a second invitation to touch her. He wrapped an arm around her and she snuggled closer.

"Guess I should have worn something a little thicker."

"I'm glad you didn't."

Her slight laugh bounced off his chest and ricocheted through his heart. He liked holding her. "Thank you for a very nice evening."

He felt her smile into his chest as she said, "I should be the one thanking you, since you bought."

"You provided the practice area," he reminded her. "And came up with a great routine."

"I cheated because I copied someone else."

"Who cares, as long as we beat the Hendersons."

Mary Ann leaned away and glanced up at him. "You don't like them, do you?"

Kyle frowned. "Not much."

"Really?" She paused, appearing surprised. "I understand why I dislike them. I can't figure out why you would too."

Even though he'd revealed too much about his past during dinner, he decided to humor her. "They remind me too much of my dad and stepmother," he said honestly. "They want the world around them to conform to them rather than conforming to the world."

"That's sad."

"Yes, it is." Kyle didn't add more and she seemed content to drop the subject.

At the entrance to her door, she turned and held out her hand. "Thanks again."

He looked at her face, taking in her eyes full of warmth, before he lowered his gaze to her hand, then raised it back to her face and shook his head. Grinning, he waved her hand away and leaned in, giving her plenty of time to resist. But she didn't. Instead, she eagerly stepped closer and wrapped her arms around him as his mouth found hers.

As before, the touch was electric when he grazed her lips with the barest connection, tasting salt on his tongue as it circled her mouth. She moaned and he deepened the kiss.

When he broke their connection, he put his chin on her head and simply held her.

She snuggled closer. "You feel good."

"So do you." He leaned back and peered down at her. "So good that I don't want to leave." Yet the vulnerability he saw in her eyes scared him shitless. Kyle distanced himself and cleared his throat. "But I think it's for the best if I do."

"I guess I'll see you Saturday." She inserted the key and pushed in the heavy door.

He held it open while she retrieved her key. Suddenly Saturday seemed a long time in the future. "Why don't I pick you up and we can have an early dinner." He winked. "My choice this time."

Mary Ann brushed strands behind her ear. "Okay. I'd like that." Once inside, she turned and offered one of her signature smiles. "Good night, Kyle."

Kyle walked away wishing he were better at long-term relationships. According to the self-help books he'd read, he was afraid of intimacy. But hell, experience had taught him to fear it.

Somehow he had to figure out a way to keep his attraction to Mary Ann buttoned tight. The biggest hurdle he had to overcome was to quit kissing her. Doing so only weakened his resolve. Every time he locked lips with her, he wanted more. If he didn't stop, he'd pass the point of no return where both of them would lose.

Chapter 7

Mary Ann clicked the mouse. The last grouping of pictures of best-selling costume jewelry pieces that Unlimited Accessories had sold in the preceding three months flashed on her computer screen before the words *The End.* Satisfied, she closed the program, then shut down her computer. The PowerPoint presentation for her project was finished and ready to go for her Monday morning meeting with the buyer who represented a chain of twenty stores. Nailing the account would ease her short-term worries about money.

Her phone rang. Glancing at the clock, she wiped her sweaty palms on her pants, reached for the phone, and sent up a brief prayer that there were no problems with shipments that would delay her leaving.

"Murphy here." At five after five, she was ready for some downtime. All three of her hourly employees had left already. She'd worked late every night this week, except the night Kyle had taken her to dinner.

"My brother is in a play and I happen to have an extra ticket. Are you game?"

The deep voice elicited a smile that settled on her face; she couldn't help it. The idea of spending any time with Kyle was a hundred times better than working. "Does this play include dinner?"

"It might."

Mary Ann leaned back in her chair and slipped out of her shoes. "Good, 'cause I'm famished."

"I know I should have given you more notice. Traffic's a nightmare. I'm still in Oakland and heading south now. We can stop for something quick on the way."

"Where is this play?"

"In the Oakland Hills. Which means we're cutting it close for the eight o'clock performance. Expect me in about twenty-five minutes."

"Oh, for heaven's sake. I can take BART and meet you in downtown Oakland." The BART station was only a five-minute walk from her office.

"You will?"

"Of course I will." Traffic was bad enough without having to backtrack during rush hour. "We're friends after all, right?" Even as she said the comment so vehemently, she had her fingers crossed. Kyle Davidson was more than a friend and as long as she had dance classes with him to look forward to on Saturday night, she would keep him as a friend. Then she remembered her plans to meet Sam for bingo and a twinge of guilt flittered into her thoughts. She discarded it quickly enough. Sam wasn't there last week, which meant she could take a break. Besides, Mary Ann's mom was always pushing her to date more. It would be best not to mention this particular date was with Kyle.

Otherwise, she might never hear the end of it. God knows, she didn't need Colleen Murphy making wedding plans for her and Kyle, like she'd done when she'd been dating Steve. Wouldn't Kyle just laugh if he knew? Of course he would, because it was funny. She sobered, because somehow the thought made her feel empty.

"Oh, and Kyle? Don't let on about tonight. Or Monday night either, unless you want my mom picking out china patterns for us," she added for good measure. Her mom meant well, but it tended to scare guys off.

As expected, he did laugh. "I won't tell her if you don't tell Irma. I cringe to think of the wedding plans the two of them could come up with if they got wind of us becoming friends."

"Lord help us if that ever happens."

"Text me when you get on BART, so I'll know what train you're on. Then let me know when you get off. I may have to circle the block a few times, but at this time of night it's easier than parking."

Holding the phone at her ear while she stuffed her briefcase, she said, "Are you sure you want to mess with it? I'm sure your brother won't mind that I'm not there."

"Maybe not, but I'll mind. See you in about an hour," he said before saying good-bye and hanging up.

Mary Ann dropped the phone into its cradle. Staring into space, she exhaled a huge sigh and hugged herself. He actually called to ask her out. She grabbed her purse, slung it over her shoulder along with her briefcase, and headed for the door, practically skipping the entire way. She felt ten years old and about to embark on an adventure.

Careful, Mary Ann. It's only a casual night out to see a middle school play. "Yes," she answered herself out loud. "But it also includes dinner." Her last shared dinner with Kyle entered her thoughts and she stuck her tongue out at her scared self. That part of her was paranoid. She didn't want to be that way any longer. So what if she'd made a mistake with Steve Henderson. He was the one at fault for leading her on, not her for falling for his BS. Yeah, but she should have seen the signs and that was one thing she couldn't ignore. Still, this was different. She vowed that if she saw any signs that things weren't what she thought, she'd bail in a heartbeat. Having already been burned, there was no sense sticking a hand right in the fire.

Kyle's car was in the exact spot he'd said it would be. Mary Ann quickly jumped in and he weaved around a few other double-parked cars.

"How was the train ride?"

"Fine." She shrugged. "Not much different than any ride, I'd expect."

"Okay, that was a stupid question." He downshifted to stop at a light, then glanced at her. "But I can't help it. I'm a little nervous."

"You?" She couldn't stop the laugh from coming out. "Sell me something else because I don't buy it."

"Is that so hard to believe?"

"Yes. The guy who danced the cha-cha in my living room is not the nervous type."

"I'm not usually. But…" He sighed and wiped his face. When his hand went back to the gearshift, he caught her gaze, his totally serious. "I like you."

"Really?" Her smile started at her toes and ended at her eyes. "I like you too." She hesitated. "Still, that's no reason to be nervous."

"Okay, the truth is I'm nervous about your meeting my family."

Her grin stretched and she patted the side of his face. "That's so cute. But you said it yourself, we're just friends and as such parental meetings are no big deal."

"You haven't met Stephie and Ronald Davidson before."

Mary Ann waved his concern away. "They have to have some redeeming qualities."

"You think the best of everyone, don't you?"

"Everyone except Steve and Taylor Henderson." She scrunched

up her nose. "I love their triplets, though. They are adorable. So cute the way they all look alike." She sat back in the seat and looked out the window as they drove through the Oakland Hills. "I bet they keep their parents up all night." She didn't add that she secretly wished for that exact scenario to provide some karmic justice in this world after all.

They pulled into the parking lot of what looked to be a private school. Glancing at the surroundings, Mary Ann figured it had to take big bucks to enroll a kid here. She whistled. "It looks a little hoity-toity for my blood," she said. "Are you sure you want me as your date?"

She looked down at her frumpy skirt and blouse. It was a trendy enough outfit, accessorized with her own designs, but judging from her surroundings, the people who attended these events probably wore designer cocktail gowns and real diamonds. Way out of her league. That had been a bone of contention between her and Steve. Suddenly it struck her that maybe there had been a few warning signs glaring in bright neon lights. She'd chosen to ignore them.

Kyle hopped out of the car and ran around to the other side, opening her door for her. She struggled to uncurl herself out of the little car, a task made easier because Kyle had pulled her to her feet. "How in the hell do you get out of that thing so quickly?"

He shrugged. "Practice." Then he grinned. "You still want to learn how to drive a clutch?"

Day was turning quickly to night. As the last rays of twilight lingered, she ran her gaze up one side of the car and down the other. In the dark it was pretty, but in what was left of the light, it was more than pretty. It was a work of art.

"I don't think I should," she said as he put his hand at the small of her back to guide her toward the entrance. His touch did something to her. Made her yearn for more than friendship. But since that was all he wanted, she planned on it being a good one. "I'd just mess it up," she said honestly, fighting to maintain her composure, which was next to impossible with him so close.

"If you ever change your mind." Sighing, he shrugged.

His hand still touching the small of her back felt hot, which was kind of weird since the wind had a tendency to rip right through her. Thankfully she'd ridden the bus to work that day, and had worn a jacket that was wind resistant.

After guiding her inside, Kyle had to grab the door to prevent the wind from blowing it into the brick wall.

"Kyle, I'm glad you made it." The strong voice came from Mary Ann's right. She turned and noted a good-looking older man in his midfifties. Though he looked nothing like Kyle, he had to be his dad, considering the kid trailing behind him. The boy quickly passed the older man, zeroing in on Kyle, and rushed up to him, locking arms around his waist. He had to be Brad, Kyle's brother. "Hey, little buddy." Kyle gave him a big hug. When he let go, he said, "Brad, this is my friend Mary Ann."

She grinned. "Good to meet you."

Brad glanced over his shoulder. "I have to go and get ready." He turned back around. "I'm really glad you could come."

"I wouldn't miss it," Kyle said to his departing back as he scampered off. At the same time a feminine voice said, "It's good to see you, Kyle."

Mary Ann jerked her attention away from the two brothers to spot a blonde woman in her mid to late forties, looking very put together, slip her arm around Kyle's father's arm.

Glancing down at her wrinkled skirt, Mary Ann groaned silently. Obviously, Kyle's stepmother never had to deal with BART. No, those expensive clothes and that two-hundred dollar haircut and color meant she probably was driven around town in a chauffeured limo oblivious to the fact that people actually had to wait in the rain for a bus, or endure hours of commuting across the bay to work every day.

When Kyle made the introductions, Stephie, as he'd called her, ignored Mary Ann's outstretched hand.

"Nice to meet you, Mary Ann," Ronald Davidson said, reaching for the hand she still had out, as if trying to offset his wife's rudeness. "Any friend of Kyle's is a friend of mine."

Mary Ann shook it, but quickly let go when she noticed Stephie's frown. Surely the woman couldn't be jealous of her? Yet vibes seldom lied, and those shooting from those cool blue eyes flared hotter.

Stephie had manicured nails that were clearly done at the most expensive salons in the Bay Area. Mary Ann knew this because the hand models her company hired for jewelry shots spent tons of money to have their nails and fingers look just so. Mary Ann glanced at her own hand and quickly put it behind her back as nonchalantly as possible, which wasn't an easy feat considering the ten dangly bracelets she wore. Her jewelry wasn't tacky, her hands were clean, and her nails clipped, but somehow she felt lacking.

"The show is starting soon," Ronald said. He turned to his wife and held out his arm. "We should take our seats."

Stephie nodded, and without saying good-bye or nice meeting you or go to hell, she allowed her husband to guide her inside the student auditorium.

"That was interesting," Mary Ann said honestly. "Did I do something to offend her?"

"No. Just ignore her." The sigh Kyle offered along with his sympathetic smile did little to ease her mind. Her gaze sought the couple now sitting at two chairs on the end row. There were two seats left on the same row to the inside of them. As Kyle once again placed his hand of the small of her back with enough pressure to get her moving, Mary Ann prayed they wouldn't have to sit next to them.

Unfortunately, prayer didn't work. Kyle stopped at their row. Ronald stood and stepped aside to let them in. Stephie simply shifted her knees, giving them barely enough room to slide by her. Not wanting to sit next to Kyle's stepmother, she sat one seat over.

"Chicken," Kyle whispered as he sat in the vacant seat next to his stepmother.

Mary Ann merely smiled and said in a low voice so only he could hear, "I know how much she means to you. I wouldn't think of depriving you of that spot."

"Thanks a lot. I'll remember that."

The room darkened as the lights faded and the curtain opened. From that point on, Mary Ann forgot about Kyle's rude stepmother and concentrated on his brother, who played an excellent Artful Dodger.

"Bravo," Mary Ann yelled, clapping, when the curtain finally closed. She'd enjoyed the show, the same as everyone else in the auditorium, judging from the applause. The lights brightened and she stood, along with Kyle and his parents.

"That was wonderful. Your son is truly gifted."

The woman actually bristled. "My son is very talented." Her body stiffened as did her smile. "And much too bright to be a lowly actor," Stephie added with her nose in the air before doing an about-face and walking toward the exit.

Ronald flashed an apologetic smile and followed her.

"Geez, if that's what you had to put up with your entire life, I really pity you," Mary Ann admitted, glancing at Kyle.

Kyle's gaze danced a jig, his amusement the music. "Now you

know something of my motivations back then for wanting to make her suffer."

"I'm glad she got a little karmic justice. Unfortunately, someone needs to put her in her place now."

"I couldn't agree more, but it's not us. We don't have to live with her." The tilt of his head indicated the rear of the auditorium. "He does." Kyle's smile grew. "Suddenly I feel a little sorry for the old man."

"I wonder how he puts up with her." She glanced at the back of the big room.

"According to Grams, my dad was lonely after my mom died."

Mary Ann turned to him and reached for his hand, giving it a reassuring squeeze. "I never realized how lucky I am to have grown up with so much love and understanding surrounding me." The Murphys may not have been able to afford to send their kids to a prestigious school like this one, but they did right by their kids. Mary Ann had had everything she needed, especially love, which you couldn't buy. Love was freely given. Kyle obviously needed some along with acceptance, and Mary Ann knew how to give it freely, without expecting anything in return.

"I had Grams," he said, leading her up the aisle. "So my childhood wasn't all bad."

Outside, they met up with Ronald and Stephie. Brad soon joined them. After rounds of congratulations, Ronald turned to Kyle. "You're more than welcome to join us."

Kyle glanced at her. Mary Ann couldn't hide the disappointment in her eyes quickly enough. His arm slid around her waist and he gave her a brief squeeze. "Thanks, but we've got plans." Kyle then addressed Brad. "You outdid yourself, bro. I was proud of you."

Brad beamed, even as his mother said something to negate the compliment. Shaking his head, Kyle simply bade his good-byes and steered Mary Ann toward his car.

His jaw had hardened to granite and his relaxed posture had become board-like as he pressed the button to unlock the car.

Minutes later as he turned onto the busy street, his voice interrupted her thoughts. "Taylor Henderson reminds me of my stepmother."

"Ah," Mary Ann said, nodding. "Now I understand." With her gaze on the passing scenery, she almost felt sorry for Steve. Almost. Then she smiled. Maybe there was karmic justice after all.

One could only hope.

"I thought we could play tourist tonight." Heading toward the water, Kyle weaved through Oakland's side streets until he parked at a lot not too far from Jack London Square. "You can decide where to eat."

Arm in arm, they walked the length of the square.

"Did you order the weather?" she asked, interrupting the companionable silence.

"Maybe," he said grinning.

There was little wind as passersby milled about, taking advantage of the clear night.

At the entrance to a trendy spot boasting of wood-fired pizza, Mary Ann stopped to peruse the menu. "This looks like a fun place."

Neither mentioned the earlier unpleasantness as they ate, and all too soon, they were back on the freeway driving south. Kyle found a spot not too far away from her building. When he moved to open his door, she put a hand on his arm to stop him.

"I can make it from here." Putting a little distance between seemed like a good idea.

"Of course you can. But since you braved BART earlier, the least I can do is walk you to your door."

The quiet night surrounded them. Yet, like earlier that evening, it was a companionable silence rather than a strained one.

At her door, Kyle held out his hand for her key. A streak of pleasure zinged up her spine over his consideration. "You really are a nice guy." And then, because she really didn't want the evening to end, she asked, "Would you like to come up for a nightcap?" When he hesitated, she said, "I still have a couple more Paulaners. You're welcome to one of them." Regrets could come later.

The sexy grin reached his serious eyes, darkened to jade with only the hall light silhouetting his face. "I'd like that."

***

Kyle unlocked the door to Mary Ann's apartment as she waited patiently. He knew damned well he shouldn't have accepted her invitation because it was getting harder and harder to remember his rule about noninvolvement. Even if he hadn't sworn off sex, the idea of starting something with Mary Ann wasn't a good one, considering their backgrounds. Hell, she was full of life and the true girl next door. She'd been raised around love and kindness all her life. Kyle couldn't remember kindness, even when his mother was alive, thanks to his father's actions after her death. Grams was always kind and loving, but Kyle craved more. Which was exactly why he did what he did with his kids. The thought stopped him. Was that his true motivation for helping them? To find some sort of acceptance?

Mary Ann's throat clearing drew him out of his thoughts. He looked up to see that she'd put her jacket away and had her hand out, obviously waiting for him to take his off.

"Sorry," he said, shrugging out of it as the heat of a flush crawled up his neck. God, blushing was for young fools. Kyle might not be young, but he was acting foolish. He had to quit thinking about Mary Ann as anything other than a friend, because he couldn't give her what any normal woman deserved. Total love and acceptance. The only person Kyle loved like that was Grams.

The thought stopped him. Mainly because it was true.

No wonder those other women had left me, he thought as more truth hit him square in the jaw. When things got to the point where he needed to pony up and deliver the love goods, Kyle didn't have any in him to give. Mary Ann had already gone through one disappointing relationship with Steve. She didn't deserve another guy who was emotionally bankrupt.

He followed Mary Ann into the kitchen. Despite her ten-date rule, everything about her was open, subconsciously telling him he could have her. All he had to do was ask. And commit, his conscience warned.

When Kyle took the beer she offered, their knuckles bumped. She almost jumped at the spark the connection created. Ignoring the reaction, he kept his attention on uncapping the bottle. As he took a long swig, he realized a beer might not be the best solution to keeping their distance.

The air sizzled with tension as she brushed her skirt. Her dangling bracelets jingled, drawing his gaze. He liked the funky jewelry she always wore; it suited her. Nothing cold like diamonds in platinum. Hers were just as shiny, but like the woman, there was a warmth to them that shouted fun.

Mary Ann swept a few stray curls behind her ear, cleared her throat, and pointed to the sofa. "Would you like to sit?"

"Sure." After getting to know her pretty well in the last week, he could tell she was nervous.

Hell, so was he. But for a different reason. He was nervous

about doing something that would ruin their friendship. Though it was only one beer, alcohol tended to stymie inhibitions that normally wouldn't allow him to act. Best to just drink and go.

"Did I do something wrong?" she asked as he swallowed another mouthful.

The unexpected question had him practically choking on the liquid going down his throat. He coughed and set the bottle in the center of a coaster resting on the table in front of him. "No." He couldn't meet her gaze as he added, "Why do you think that?"

"Oh, I don't know. Maybe because you won't look me in the eyes."

He risked a glance in her direction. Wrong thing to do. The acceptance he glimpsed had his pulse racing and his palms sweating. He wiped them on his pants and reached for his beer. In three gulps, he polished it off. Then he stood.

When she did likewise, he handed her his empty bottle. "I'd better go."

"You just got here," she said in an accusing voice. "I did do something wrong, didn't I?"

"No." He grabbed her shoulders when she was about to apologize again for something that was neither of their faults. "You didn't do anything but be who you are."

"Then why are you leaving?"

"Because I think it would be foolish of me to stay." He looked her directly in the eye without bothering to hide the need that suddenly overtook him the moment he touched her.

"Oh," she said with a loud gasp. She quickly averted her gaze and shuffled her feet, as if uncomfortable. "I see."

"You deserve more than I can give," he murmured, lifting her chin. Keeping his eyes open and ignoring her wide-eyed stare, he leaned in and kissed her. Then, his bad sense overtook his good and he closed his eyes, savoring what he'd refused himself all evening. God, she smelled like a garden after a rainstorm. Fresh and clean, and she tasted the same.

Kyle deepened the kiss, opening his mouth wider when she wrapped her arms around him to draw him closer. His body responded and he couldn't stop what grew between them. As if he'd burned her, she pulled away. Red highlighted her features as she nodded. "I definitely see now."

He smiled, gave her one more kiss, and headed for the door. "I'll pick you up tomorrow night before class."

"You don't have to. I can drive myself."

He stopped with his hand on the doorknob and glanced back at her. "It's only fair because you took BART this afternoon." He shut the door behind him, not willing to admit why he'd offered. He liked being with her. Time spent driving back and forth was at least some compensation when he couldn't have her.

***

Mary Ann stared at the closed door, wondering why her apartment seemed so empty. She sat back down on the couch and reached for her beer. As she took a sip, she fought to regain her sanity. Kissing Kyle was like some kind of drug that messed with her willpower. The instant she'd felt his need, everything inside her wanted to respond.

Before she met Kyle, she hadn't wanted a relationship. Unfortunately, she wasn't the type to have an affair. It was as clear as the nose on her face. An affair was all he could offer. Worse, he wasn't offering it to her.

Still clutching the half-full bottle, she rose and headed for her bedroom, telling herself Kyle was right. She did deserve more.

If that were so, then why was she counting the seconds until tomorrow's class?

Chapter 8

True to his word, Kyle picked Mary Ann up in plenty of time to make their dance class.

They entered the studio to Frau Haubner's clapping.

"Listen up, class!"

Already at it, he thought, wishing the sound weren't so brittle, as both he and Mary Ann stopped to hear her announcement.

"We are in store for a treat," she said in her usual manner of pronouncing her *Ws* like *Vs*. "The couple who joined us late has had two private lessons to make up for missing last week's class. They have volunteered to help anyone who has trouble with their cha-cha."

Everyone in the class, including Mary Ann and Kyle, turned to the back of the room and noted the good-looking couple dressed to the nines tonight. Henderson wore a suit that wasn't off the rack, and Taylor's evening gown looked expensive enough to be a Paris original. It astounded him that the couple would try to use clothing as a means of setting themselves apart from the masses in this class. Kyle couldn't believe there were others on the planet who could be as condescending as his father, or rather, his father's wife.

When he felt Mary Ann stiffen, he turned to her and whispered, "What's wrong?"

"I will let you practice for another five minutes," Frau Haubner announced, her *will* sounding like *vill*. "Then we will move on, *ja?*"

Mary Ann flashed him an annoyed grimace. "Nothing's wrong."

He glanced back at the overdressed couple. "You don't think we can outdo them?"

"Of course we'll outdo them!" She grabbed his arm. "Let's practice it one more time, then show this crowd how to dance."

They went through the routine perfectly the first time without the music. When she was about to go again, Kyle shook his head. "We don't want to over-practice or jinx anything."

He glanced toward the snooty couple executing a decent cha-

cha and clenched his fist. His jaw tightened. For some reason, he wanted to wipe their butts across the dance floor. He refocused on Mary Ann and caught her watching them. She turned to look at him, wearing a mask of indifference. But he knew her well enough to spot the doubt in her eyes. She didn't believe they could do it. Well, he was the leader and he'd lead them to a convincing win today, or else.

Why it mattered, he really didn't know. He only knew that something inside him hated to see her unhappy. Steve and Taylor winning fit that bill.

Another clap brought the practice session to an end.

"Who wants to go first?"

"We will," said a man a few feet away. "Might as well get it over with," he joked. The rest of the class laughed and Frau Haubner put on the music.

A fast-paced cha-cha sounded and the couple began dancing to the beat. "They aren't half bad," Kyle whispered to Mary Ann, who stood next to him.

Other couples braved the floor and soon there were only two couples left. Kyle and Mary Ann, and the Hendersons.

Frau Haubner looked directly at Kyle. Her stern voice sounded like an order. "Your turn."

"Showtime," he said under his breath.

Mary Ann grabbed his hand and squeezed. "Thanks for being my partner."

Still, he caught lingering doubt in her gaze and shook his head. "Wait until after we win before you thank me." He winked. "Just follow my lead."

Grinning, she shot back, "I'd follow you anywhere."

At least the earlier doubt was gone, but her statement didn't sit well because he sensed she meant every word.

When the music began again, Kyle let it guide him, following the steps he and Mary Ann had practiced. She was livelier tonight, her smile beckoning him to lead her astray. She was saucy to his swagger.

The beat took over and suddenly it was more than a dance.

Mary Ann was the one he wanted and he was doing his best to capture her. When their ninety seconds were up, applause drew him out of his stupor. He was hard as stone and wanted her with a passion he'd never known before. He glanced into her eyes. Her emotions mirrored his.

He couldn't mistake that look, and somehow he let her go and stepped away. How in the hell did those guys on the show dance so professionally? If they felt half of what he'd felt, they had to be aroused more than a little, especially considering those skimpy costumes the women wore. Thank God for wool trousers and boxer briefs. He adjusted himself so as not to create more of a spectacle.

"That was wonderful." Mary Ann hugged him. He was careful to keep enough space between them so she wouldn't know.

Thankfully, the music started again and the Hendersons took to the floor, doing a cha-cha that appeared as intricate as theirs had been.

Having fully recovered, Kyle swore under his breath. He hated the couple even more, if that were possible. They looked so in synch with each other. He hadn't been able to tell if he and Mary Ann had been in synch, too absorbed in dancing to pay much attention.

"Bravo," Frau Haubner said as she bent to turn off the sound system. "Will you please come up here?"

The Hendersons practically gloated in their victory. Until Frau Haubner glanced at him and said, "You and your partner, too."

Shocked, Kyle put his hand on his heart, pointing to himself. Frau Haubner smiled. "Yes, you. And your pretty partner." Her nod indicated the front of the room where the Hendersons still stood, although now they didn't appear quite so smug.

Kyle glanced at Mary Ann with eyebrows lifted. "After you," he said, holding out his hand.

Wearing the biggest grin he'd ever seen, Mary Ann hurried to stand next to Steve. Kyle figured she was dying to stick her tongue out at him, and he had to admit, he had a similar urge.

The instructor joined them at the front of the studio. She turned to the class. "These two couples embody everything dance is about. If we could take the best from each and join them, we'd have perfection."

She pointed to the Hendersons. "Here we have perfect technique. Can anyone tell me what was missing from their performance?"

When no one spoke up she moved closer to Kyle. "They lacked what this team has in abundance. *Passion*." She paused for effect. "What this couple lacked in technique, they made up for in *passion*." She emphasized the one word. Twice.

After an audible exhale, Frau Haubner turned to the Hendersons. "You need more passion. Without it, technique is wasted."

Though the dragon lady was implying their technique needed improvement, Kyle felt ten feet tall. They had passion. Of course they had passion; he'd felt it from the first moment Mary Ann had placed her hand in his. Maybe that was why those guys on TV could dance with other couples. Talent had them creating the passion. With Mary Ann it was just there.

The rest of the class was arduous because they were learning a waltz, and the waltz hold was tighter than the cha-cha. Kyle had never been one to let the music sway him, but gliding on the floor with Mary Ann following his lead was intoxicating as hell. He finally understood why ballroom dancing was so popular in bygone days. It was a prelude to sex, almost like foreplay. At least for him it was. Excruciatingly sexy—the movements exaggerating every sense.

By the end of the class, Kyle knew he was in big trouble.

In silence they drove south on the Nimitz to the Hayward exit. He slowed on her street, and double-parked in front of her building.

In his present mood, he wasn't sure he could follow through with his determination to keep things from escalating if he didn't get the hell away from here. He wanted her too much.

"I'll call you during the week and we can talk about our next practice. Only he couldn't look at her as he added, "Thanks for a nice time. I enjoyed it."

***

Mary Ann jumped out of the car after it was clear that Kyle wasn't going to open her door like he usually did. It didn't matter, she told herself on her way inside. She was a big girl who could open her own doors, thank you very much. Yet as she climbed the stairs to her apartment, a part of her was disappointed he'd declined her offer to fix something to eat. She knew full well why. Heavens, how could she not? Considering all those times during the course of the evening when the heat of his erection had scorched her after accidently touching her? She'd pegged them as accidents because when it happened that first time at the end of their cha-cha and she'd all but gone up in flames, Kyle had clearly avoided contact afterward.

If only she were the type of girl to have a fling!

Dreamily, Mary Ann waltzed her way into her apartment and then into the kitchen, suddenly hungry. She grabbed her cell phone and texted Sam. *Sorry about last night. Are you busy now?*

Mary Ann typed in full sentences. She never used abbreviations. Knowledge was power, and the minute a person slacked off in using what knowledge they'd acquired was the height of laziness in her mind.

Her cell phone jingled. Grinning, Mary Ann answered. "Hey, Sam. I'm not interrupting anything, am I?"

"Not a thing. James is at the office so I'm dateless. Want to grab a bite? I can drive over the bridge and we can go to Mario's."

"Sure thing. Call me when you're outside my building and I'll come right down."

"Will do," Sam said before adding a good-bye.

Cutting the connection, Mary Ann paced, filled with a sudden energy. Thank God for Sam. She didn't want to stay cooped up in her small apartment. The walls were closing in on her. And worse, she couldn't excise their cha-cha and the feel of Kyle's arousal from her thoughts. It's only sex, she murmured, grabbing a coat twenty minutes later after receiving Sam's call. Besides, sex had been rather dull with Steve, so why couldn't she stop thinking about making love with Kyle?

She climbed into Sam's car. "Thanks for coming to my rescue."

"Is that what I'm doing?"

"Yes," she admitted. Sam would eventually drag it out of her. This way, they could spend more time talking about why she was obsessing about Kyle. "And you know so." She fastened her seat belt into place. As Sam veered away from the curb, Mary Ann started talking, filling her in on the last eight days, which took the entire time they drove to Mario's.

Wonderful scents of garlic and fresh-baked bread wafted past her nose when they neared the entrance. A local chain, Mario's was always a boisterous, crowded place alive with atmosphere, complete with checkered tablecloths and lit candles in straw-covered Chianti wine bottles on every table.

It was Saturday night and the restaurant seemed more rowdy than usual as the two pushed farther inside. Mario's was Sam's favorite pizza chain.

"I'll buy the first round," Sam said, pulling her out of her thoughts. "If you put our name on the waiting list."

"Sure." She turned to give the hostess her name as Sam jostled her way in the direction of the bar to order beers. By the time she was able to join Sam, her friend had already staked out a couple of seats and now held two frosty mugs filled with the house special.

Mary Ann slid onto the bar stool and rested her feet on the bottom rung. "So, what do you suggest I do?" She almost had to yell to be heard over the din. It was a good thing she'd unloaded her problem on the way over. She'd forgotten how noisy the bar could be. The restaurant part was much quieter.

"I'd seduce him."

She practically choked on the sip of beer she'd just taken. "I'm serious," she said when she could finally talk.

"What?" Sam stared at her like she'd grown an extra head. "Why not?" she asked, her expression turning more solemn. "You like him." She shrugged and picked up her beer. Before taking a draft, she added, "It's obvious he likes you. Go for it."

Closing her eyes, Mary Ann shook her head. "I don't think I can."

"What do you mean, you don't think you can?" Sam pretended to look all around her. "Where's the Mary Ann who used to take guys by storm?" She snorted. "Before Steve came into the picture, you were much more confident."

"Maybe," she said, sighing. "But I've still never seduced anyone." She had to be in a committed relationship before she'd make love. "And since college, no one's really excited me until Steve. I really thought he was 'the one,' you know?"

"Yeah." Sam's grin was infectious. "Just like I thought Charles was the one."

Mary Ann laughed. "I never liked that guy." She scrunched up her nose.

"I never liked Steve, so we're even." Sam paused to take another drink, then set her mug back down on the bar with a plunk that blended with the noise around them. "Tell me more about Kyle."

"Excuse me," said a male voice. Mary Ann leaned back as the guy next to her reached for a napkin from the holder directly in front of her.

"Thanks." The attractive guy nodded, his smile telling her he'd buy her the next round if she were willing to chat. She wasn't, but it dawned on her exactly what Sam was implying. Maybe she had cut herself off from life as her mother had said.

Even if she got back out there as everyone kept telling her to do, she still couldn't seduce a man simply for sex. It simply wasn't in her nature. She wasn't a prude, but she wasn't into indiscriminant sex either. Sam began extolling the pluses of what could happen if she took the bull by the horns. In this case, it would be Kyle's erection, not a bull, Sam corrected as the pager on the bar lit up and a buzzing noise made the little contraption dance.

"Thank God our table is ready." Mary Ann picked up the vibrating pager and glanced at Sam, relieved by the interruption. "I'm starved."

Sam followed her as the two wound their way through the crowd. "Don't think I'm letting this go. It's obvious you like this guy and he likes you. Why shouldn't you be the one to take the initiative?"

She spun around. "Because..." but closed her mouth when she had no ready answer.

"I did it and looked what happened to me!" Presenting a smug smile, Sam took the chair the waitress had pulled out and sat. "James was the last person on earth who was ready for a relationship, but he fell in love. And the rest is history."

"Yeah." Mary Ann grabbed her own chair and plopped into it, wishing it didn't make some sort of sense. "I guess I'm scared. What if he rejects me?"

Flipping open her menu, Sam leaned forward. "Now you're letting that shithead Steve rule your thoughts. Would you have thought about trying before Steve?" She then focused on the menu in her hand.

Mary Ann grinned. "Actually, I did give Steve a little push." Although why Sam even bothered to look at a menu when she always ordered the same thing was beyond her. She perused her own, adding, "Amazing what a little wine and a nice meal could do for a guy's libido." Still, it hadn't been very exciting. Steve had been finished before she even got warmed up. After that it got better, but not much. "What if it doesn't lead to a relationship?"

"Sounds to me like you already have a relationship. Are you so scared that you're not willing to take a chance?" Sam frowned. "Just because you have a ring on your finger doesn't mean it will last. Nowadays fifty percent of marriages fail, and I'll bet if you asked those couples about their relationship, they'd swear on a stack of bibles they were committed when they got married. Some commitment, huh?"

"That's even more depressing." Married thirty-five years, her parents were in the minority.

Their waitress walked up and the two ordered.

"Commit yourself to giving it a go," Sam said as she walked away. "I'd be willing to bet, considering what you've told me, this Kyle is just as afraid of commitment as you are."

"I'm not afraid of commitment."

"Then why would you pick a jerk like Steve as your knight in shining armor? Kyle seems much more suited to the title and you're not even willing to try."

She swallowed hard and thought about what Sam had just said. "Geez," she whispered, brushing a strand of unruly hair behind her ears. "When you put it like that, it makes some kind of karmic sense."

"Attraction's a wonderful thing. Use it to your benefit and don't think about what-ifs."

Mary Ann trailed a finger on her silverware as her mind spun. She smiled, thinking of earlier that night. Maybe Kyle was afraid of his own feelings. What Mary Ann felt scared her to death, and the idea of following through on finding out what could happen scared her more. But Sam was right. She couldn't let Steve's rejection ruin her sense of self any more than she'd already allowed him to.

When the pizza came, Mary Ann reached for a slice of the meaty, cheesy pie. She barely tasted all the wonderful flavors, too intent on making her plans for seduction. With only four more weeks of lessons, each and every waking hour counted.

Chapter 9

With the last report finally done, Kyle dropped the pen and leaned back in the plush leather chair. For hours, he'd worked to clear up minor expenses from his last job. He rolled his shoulders to ease the stiffness of slumping over a desk doing paperwork, something he hated. Rarely and only when absolutely necessary did he work in the office.

His gaze traveled to the wall of windows that faced San Francisco Bay from the Oakland side. The only nice thing about being cooped up in the office allocated to him was the view. He turned and looked out the other wall of windows facing the inner fourth floor of Davidson Construction. What was supposed to have been a couple of months had turned into two years. He stayed on as a silent partner simply because he had the freedom to run the business as he pleased, as if he still owned his old company, which was now a subsidiary of Davidson Construction.

Kyle's phone whistled, indicating a text. He glanced down at the device in his hand. A thrill shot through him at seeing Mary Ann's name appear on the small screen. Then his body tensed. Maybe she was canceling their practice session.

Got a nasty cold. Don't feel like practicing tonight.

The disappointment that followed didn't mean anything. Winning the dance competition was a goal and without practice, they didn't stand a chance. That's all, he reasoned.

Need some chicken soup? he texted back.

A smiley face appeared. Glancing at it, Kyle tried to figure out if her answer was a yes or a no.

He stood and headed out the door, deciding to interpret it his way. She wanted TLC and he meant to give it to her.

First stop was the soup shop a block away from the office building. Kyle ordered enough for two and was soon in his car and heading south.

Though rush hour, he made the drive relatively quickly, then wended his way through Hayward's streets and parked.

Kyle emerged, and tucking their dinner close to his side, he strode at a fast pace toward her apartment building's entrance.

Now at the wall of buttons, he pressed Mary Ann's and waited. "Yes?"

"I come bearing gifts."

"Is that you, Kyle?"

"Yeah. Let me in, will you. Soup's getting cold."

After a long pause, she said, "I'm not presentable."

His grin was quick. "I know. You're sick. I'm here to take care of you. Make sure you eat. You'll need your strength to get better. So we can practice," he added for good measure, so she wouldn't think he was being sappy, which he was. Still, they were friends. And friends did nice things for each other. Kyle refused to believe it was anything more.

The buzzer at the door sounded and he hurried to open it. He took the stairs two at a time, making sure their meal stayed intact.

When he knocked, Mary Ann opened her door and peeked out. She brushed back bed-head hair. "I look horrible." She wrapped her terrycloth robe closer to her middle and retied the sash. The navy color brought out the blue tint of her hazel eyes. But she looked pale, which made her nose look redder.

He grinned. "You do look like a mess, but in a cute way." He held up his bag. "You'll feel better after eating." Used to women dressed to the nines, he rather liked seeing her like this. It made her seem more human, and more like the girl next door he found so attractive.

Mary Ann stepped back and he swept past her. Glancing around, his grin widened. Her place reminded him of her.

When she bent to pick up a sock on the floor, he stopped her with a hand on her arm. "Don't worry about straightening up. I'm a guy. Which means, I tend to be more comfortable with clutter."

As she straightened, his gaze stalked her hand, now pushing strands of that gorgeous long hair behind her ear. Even tousled, he had to squelch the urge to touch it.

He trailed behind her as she headed toward the contemporary table with matching chairs he'd sat at the last time they'd practiced. Her dining area was near the bay window overlooking the street below. The draperies were still open tonight.

"Not much of a view," she said, obviously noting where his focus had drifted. Mary Ann cleared her throat. "But it is mine."

"I like it." Kyle placed the bag on the wooden tabletop. He

took the bowls of soup out of the bag along with the salad, and bread, still warm to the touch.

"Do you like butter on your bread?" When she nodded, he buttered it with the plastic knife. He set the other plastic utensils out, one each for her with napkin and one each for him.

Kyle glanced at her. "Dinner is served, my lady." He bowed first, then pulled out a chair.

"Why thank you, kind sir," she said, her formal tone matching his. She sat.

They ate in silence, one interrupted every now and then with her sniffling, followed by her blowing her nose.

"God, I'm a mess, but this is so good." Mary Ann brushed back another handful of hair. "I'm glad you brought it because it's hitting the spot. All I have in my fridge is milk and Pepsi, and I didn't feel like going to the store."

The smile she offered him, red nose and all, was like a punch in the gut. He couldn't help but return it. Though he was starting to question his motive for coming to her rescue, he was really glad he did.

***

Mary Ann scooped out the last sip of chicken noodle soup, then finished her salad, using the bread to sop up the bit of dressing still on the bottom of the throwaway container. She dropped her fork and sighed. "That hit the spot. Thanks." Of course she looked like death warmed over, which didn't aid in her quest for seduction.

Kyle had stated they were friends. Did he do things like coming to her aid for all of his friends? She sighed, wondering about the women he'd dated. He didn't seem to be a workaholic, nor did he seem to be emotionally unavailable. She shrugged, unable to figure it out.

"Thanks for dinner." She pushed away from the table, then started cleaning up.

Kyle stood and stilled her hand. "Let me do that." The tilt of his head indicated her sofa, where the blanket she'd huddled under all day still lay in disarray. "You just go and lie back down over there."

She did as he ordered. After settling herself in and wrapping herself in the blanket, she glanced up to see him standing not two feet in front of her. Smiling, she held up the remote. "I'm all set to watch *Dancing with the Stars*."

"Oh?" His eyebrows lifted in question.

"Yeah, this is the show before they pick the finalists." Knowing he'd say no, she offered, "You can stay and watch if you want. Three couples are doing the waltz," she said, adding nonchalantly, "Who knows. We might learn something." Why would anyone expose themselves to her cold?

"Okay." He made a gesture with his hand. "Scoot over."

Ignoring the burst of pleasure that shot through her, she moved closer to the armrest. "I'm taping it, so you don't have to stay," she said, giving Kyle an out. Steve surely wouldn't. Heck, he'd seldom even called when she got sick. It was most unnerving and Mary Ann didn't know how to interpret Kyle's kindness. Was he being just a friend? Or was there more to it?

Unfortunately, Kyle didn't leave, sat down instead, and she couldn't summon the will to send him away. Besides, she reasoned, running a hand through her straggling hair, she was anything but attractive right now. He was only being his usual nice self.

Kyle sat at the other end of the sofa, slipped his leather loafers off, and stretched out his legs. "Wouldn't you be more comfortable lying down?"

Wondering if he'd lost his marbles, she looked at him. Her thoughts must have shown on her face because his sly grin appeared and he patted his lap. "I promise not to ravish you."

She laughed. "Ah, an ulterior motive for aiding the damsel in distress." She swallowed her disappointment because she was too sick for seduction. "I'll have to watch you, Mr. Davidson."

"Kyle," he said, his grin widening. He patted his lap again. "Come on and get comfortable and let's see what this show has to offer tonight. We'll need all the help we can get if we expect to win."

Both settled in to watch as Max and his partner, some celebrity he'd never heard of, danced.

"Wow," Kyle said when they finished. "They can dance."

"Yeah." Mary Ann smiled. "Max is pretty good." Her smile turned dreamy. "So is Derrick."

"He's the clean-cut kid, right?"

"Um-hmm." She sighed. "Isn't he cute?"

"If you like blonds."

She could almost believe he was joking, except for the bit of sarcasm in his voice. "With a body like that, who cares?" she shot back.

"What?" His head snapped in her direction and he sought her gaze.

Mary Ann only shrugged and looked away, hiding her smile. "Guys aren't the only gender who finds bodies of the opposite sex attractive," she said, adding to her teasing.

"What about mine?" His question drew her gaze again. Eyeing her intently, he asked, "Do you find me attractive?"

She sniffled, wishing she didn't have a cold. "We're getting off subject here."

"You're right. Besides, it was a stupid question. I guess seeing all those studs dancing on the screen gave me a bit of a complex."

She studied him through half-lidded eyes. "Fishing for compliments?"

"And if I were?" His gaze turned darker and something sparked in those green eyes. "Would you compliment me?"

A forced laugh came out. "Sell me something else." Deciding she was treading too close to the edge of disaster, she leaned back and closed her eyes. She felt too miserable to think about seduction. It didn't help that she looked her worst.

"Go to sleep." She felt his soft caress on her face. Her sigh came out in one long exhale. As more relaxation set in, a soft smile settled over her face. What would it be like to feel like this all the time? Maybe this was what Steve felt was missing from their relationship. Did he have that with Taylor? She frowned at the thought.

His light touch smoothed the frown away. "You're thinking too much. Relax and go to sleep."

***

Kyle was in deep shit. None of his other girlfriends had gotten sick, and the fact that Mary Ann had and had let him comfort her did something to his soul. He liked the feeling he got from being needed. *Just like my kids*, he thought. Like popcorn popping, the burst of insight filled him, the thought expanding from a seed into the puffed-out kernel that had him questioning his motives.

A soft snore brought him back to the present and he glanced down to study her features. Devoid of makeup, a rosy Rudolph nose in the middle, her face was remarkable for being unremarkable. That wan complexion didn't mar the girl-next-door look he'd come to love.

She reminded him of old videos he'd seen of his mother. The

thought brought him up short. He swiped a hand over his face and swore under his breath. He had to get out of here before his memories played any more tricks on him. Gently, so as not to wake Mary Ann, he slipped out from beneath her head, replacing his lap with a pillow. She murmured something that sounded like a thank-you, which drew his gaze back to her face. He leaned down and kissed her on the forehead. "Don't mention it. Go back to sleep. I'll see myself out."

Chapter 10

Mary Ann's cell phone jingled, and a thrill climbed up her spine when Kyle's name appeared on the small screen.

"Hi, Kyle. What's up?"

"I'm sorry I have to beg off practicing tonight."

A surge of disappointment swamped her great mood when her attempt to arrange another practice session was met with, "I can't. I'm stretched as it is."

She frowned. Maybe Kyle was a workaholic, like he'd warned. "I guess we'll have to wing it."

He apologized again and when he made no offer to pick her up before class, she sighed. "I understand. I'll see you on Saturday."

After saying their good-byes and disconnecting the call, Mary Ann struggled to maintain a positive attitude. How could she seduce him if he was avoiding her? She wondered if his visit during her nasty cold had anything to do with the cancellation. She texted Sam to ask her opinion, then reached for a necklace that needed a bit more work.

About to shove away from the worktable with completed necklace in hand, Mary Ann stopped when her cell phone whistled, indicating a text.

Recognizing Sam's number, she quickly brought it up. Seconds later, her phone rang.

"Thanks for calling me back," Mary Ann said, going on to explain what had happened. "I'm not sure if he's really working or avoiding me because I was sick." Which didn't sound like Kyle at all.

"Or maybe he's afraid of his emotions," Sam said. "Let me find out about his schedule."

"Don't let on that I'm curious."

Sam laughed. "Don't worry. Maggie's already confided in me about keeping her fingers crossed for you two. I'll beat her at her own game and pretend like I'm the one who is interested."

"Thanks, Sam."

A knock on the door drew her attention. "Gotta go. Talk to you later," she said as Lindy, one of her sales associates, stuck her head inside.

"Mrs. Hobbs is here."

Mary Ann smiled. Right on schedule. At least some things are going well, she thought, heading toward the showroom.

"I just now finished this design." She placed the necklace on a white jeweler's pad so it would show off the black onyx and silver running throughout the piece.

"'Oh, my," Mrs. Hobbs said, fingering the piece reverently. "It's stunning."

"Would you like to try it on?" Mary Ann grasped an end with each hand and held it up.

Mrs. Hobbs immediately pulled her hair out of the way. "Yes, but this old dress won't do it justice." The elderly woman glanced in the mirror as Mary Ann placed it around her neck and fastened the clasp.

"It lays beautifully." Mrs. Hobbs reached into her bag for her wallet. "I think I'll wear it home," she said, handing over a charge card.

Mary Ann rang up the sale and handed the woman her receipt. "Enjoy it."

"Oh, honey, I will. I'll cherish my friends' envious stares." She picked up her bag with the empty display box, leaned closer, and whispered, "Don't worry. I'll be sure to mention where I got it so they can come in and have their own one-of-a-kind creation made."

Exactly what Mary Ann counted on. Word-of-mouth extra business. She smiled. A few more new customers, along with the order she'd nailed a week ago, would certainly help with her bottom line. She'd be in the black in no time.

"I have paperwork to finish," she said to Lindy, turning toward the back room. "I'll be working with Suzy and Misty on our First Impressions order." She needed to show them what designs to start working on. "Call me if you need me."

Satisfied her two associates had a handle on what they were doing, she stretched.

Her cell phone rang as she headed toward her tiny office. As she sat behind her desk, she clicked the phone on and brought the device to her ear. Doing away with a greeting because curiosity had chewed a hole in her gut, she asked, "Did you learn anything?"

A quick laugh preceded Sam's, "Hello to you, too."

Chagrined, she grunted. "Quit stalling and talk."

"Jeez, some people have no patience." She hesitated before adding a cheerful, "You do know patience is a virtue."

"Sam," Mary Ann warned.

Another laugh sounded. "Okay, okay. Don't go all schoolteacher on me," Sam said, tsk-tsking. "Apparently he's out of the office, but there are no pressing projects, according to his secretary. Maggie spoke to Irma, and she thinks he may be with his kids."

"He has kids?"

"I'm not sure what that meant, and I didn't want to ask because questions might send up red flags."

Unfortunately, Mary Ann couldn't ask either. "Thanks. I appreciate your help." Worse, she had no idea how to find it out without giving away her hand. Her only alternative was to keep to her plans for seduction, using the dance class to her best advantage. Hopefully, she wouldn't make a fool of herself in the process.

***

Frau Haubner clapped her hands and her frown could scare little kids on Halloween. "Where is the passion from last week?" she asked for the tenth time in over an hour.

Kyle didn't want her to know the passion was still there, but he was keeping a tight rein on it so it wouldn't get loose. If it did, he wasn't sure he could put it back in the corral, so to speak.

He glanced at Mary Ann, who only shook her head. She hadn't been any help at all in the first half of the class, invading the space he tried to keep between them at every opportunity. Besides not exhibiting any passion, he'd stepped on her toes at least hundred times in the last ten minutes.

"Take five," Frau Haubner said in a resigned tone, still grimacing at him. "I will work with the Hendersons."

"Are you going to let them win?" Mary Ann placed her hands on her hips and judging by the exasperation in her voice, she was annoyed with his evasive tactics. "I never wanted to compete until you decided we should. And now that I do, you're chickening out."

"It's not like that and you know it," he hissed, his voice just as annoyed. Hell, being near her for over an hour and trying not imagine her naked was taking its toll on his patience. A man could only endure so much temptation, and Kyle was at the breaking point.

"What I know is we didn't practice last week and now we have no passion."

Her imitation of Frau Haubner was spot-on, down to the *V* she used in place of her *W*. He smiled. "We have plenty of passion, and you're well aware of that fact."

"Then what's the problem?" She moved a step closer, leaning her head so that he had to look into those big round eyes. Her spicy scent rose up to taunt him further. She'd tied her hair back, but that didn't ease his desire to run his fingers through it. Kyle closed his eyes and fought harder to ignore her.

"In case you haven't realized it, big boy, they are her pets now." The tilt of her head indicated the dragon lady instructing the Hendersons. When the woman laughed, Mary Ann's gaze practically spewed fire. "Kyle, I want to beat them even if you don't, and to win we need to practice."

Kyle continued watching the two eagerly trying to suck up to Frau Haubner. They really needed some competition to bring them down a peg. But even as the thought struck, he grasped it wasn't the real reason he was about to relent. "Okay, but we should do it at the church." He did want to be with her, so it seemed like a great idea. "It has a big enough space. Plus, the people around will be an added protection," he said, not realizing he'd spoken this last bit out loud.

"That's so sweet," she practically purred, running a hand up and down his face. She patted it. "What makes you think I need or want protection?"

He gripped her hand, propelling her with him around the corner. Out of sight of the others, he pushed her against the wall, then proceeded to kiss her, drinking from her lips like a man in the desert who hasn't had water in days. When the erection he had no control over made contact with her body, something that clearly no longer shocked her, he broke the connection and looked down at her. "That's why," he ground out, trying to untangle himself from the obvious mess he'd created with his demonstration as her short laugh mocked him.

"I consider that an added benefit." She then reached around his arms and reeled him in for another knockout kiss. When she finally let him go, he lifted his head. The siren's smile plastered on her face should have been a warning, along with the way she viewed him through half-lidded eyes. She was sexy as hell, and Kyle had never wanted anyone like he wanted her.

"How's that for passion?" She lifted a brow, her tone challenging. "Would you like another demonstration?"

He smothered the urge to grin. Damn if she didn't amuse him and frustrate him at the same time. Why was he denying himself? Suddenly he couldn't quite remember, until his conscience reared its ugly head. If the lady had any idea about the battle taking place inside his brain, she'd run for her life. But she didn't, and he was beginning to realize he liked this Mary Ann as much as he liked the other one who'd warned him about their matchmakers.

That was it! He'd mention something to Grams, who'd pass the information along. Soon, Mary Ann would be avoiding him like pigeon droppings at Jack London Square.

Thankfully, the class finally ended. As Kyle walked toward his car, Mary Ann hurried up to him.

"I'm ready for my clutch lesson," she said when he stopped and turned to her with the question in his eyes.

"Now?" The woman was full of surprises.

She nodded. "Yes, now. You offered."

"I did, but I distinctly remember your declining my kind offer."

"Are you afraid of being alone in the car with me?" The sparkle in her eyes added to the dare, when she should be the one to fear what could happen.

After another mental battle, one his conscience lost, he hit the silver button on the passenger side. He opened her door. "Get in."

She waited until he seated himself and started the car before saying, "I thought you were going to teach me."

"Not here," he said, glancing in his rearview mirror and backing out of the space. He wound his way out of the parking lot and onto the busy street. "We'll go somewhere else, where there isn't as much traffic. Plus, I don't think you'll be ready for hills anytime soon. I'd rather not burn out my clutch in the first year of my car's life."

"Such a romantic," she said, grinning.

He chuckled. Yeah, he was a romantic, all right. The only thing on his mind was getting her out of those tight jeans and sweater she wore. He'd cringed every time she'd wiggled that cute butt in front of him during the last two hours. She seemed to know exactly what she was doing. "You're not trying to seduce me, are you?" It was a ridiculous notion, considering her girl-next-door persona.

"Is it working?"

Not expecting her blatant admission, he kept his focus on the road ahead, mulling it over in his brain. Worse, he had to continually remind himself why he was denying himself. Yet the reminder now lacked conviction, mainly because of her latest taunt.

He pulled into a large industrial parking lot not too far away from his grandmother's house. "Let's switch sides and I'll give you the first lesson."

She didn't hesitate, simply hopped out before he had a chance to jump out and open her door.

Once in the driver's seat, she glanced at him and he spotted nervousness in her feisty gaze. "You're not nervous?" he goaded.

"No, but I need to know what to do."

"To start the car, you need to engage the clutch and push that button, but make sure you keep your foot on the brake too."

"Like this," she said, maneuvering her feet.

"Exactly." He gave her a quick rundown on how a manual transmission worked. She soaked up every word like a vacuum cleaner sucked up dirt. "Understand?"

When she nodded, he pointed to the START button. "Go ahead, you've seen me do it."

Pursing her lips in concentration, she pushed the START button and the car's engine came alive, then settled into a quiet purr.

"Next comes the tricky part. Getting the footwork down to where you disengage the clutch after you've shifted into gear, all while giving her a little gas to get her moving."

Mary Ann followed his instructions to the letter, until she let the clutch out too quickly. The car lurched and died.

"I'm sorry."

He placed a hand on her arm and squeezed reassuringly. "No need to be sorry, just do it again. Only this time, when you feel it disengage, give it more gas." On her next try, she went all the way across the parking lot before the car lurched, and only because she tried to shift into a higher gear.

"I never realized how hard this is." She pushed in the clutch and prepared to start the car again. "If I'd have known, I'd have given you the respect you deserve."

Kyle shook his head. "Keep practicing."

"You're not afraid I'll wreck your car?"

Shrugging, he sighed. "What's a new clutch?"

"Hah," she said, glaring at him. "Watch. I'll learn and you won't have to replace a thing." For over an hour she kept at it, concentrating on maintaining the car's momentum while speeding up and climbing the gears. She made it all the way to third gear by the time he called it quits. Her determination of trying to get it right earned his respect.

"You've done well. How about a glass of wine and dessert?" With his hand on the door latch, he glanced at her. "You interested?"

Mary Ann's slow grin formed, then quickly evolved into a sly smile. "Of course," she said in a flirty voice. "I never turn down dessert if someone else is buying."

***

They spent the next hour talking about anything and everything.

"So you're a runner?" Kyle asked when she mentioned running in the Bay to Breakers race.

"Yep. My job keeps me pretty busy and I like to stay in shape. I like running because all I have to do is put on my shoes and head out the door. Twenty or thirty minutes later, I've had a good workout. Plus it keeps the extra weight off."

His gaze narrowed. "You're not one of those who diets all the time, are you?"

Her rich laughter filled the air. "Are you kidding? With these hips? Thank God running is good for something, because I love to eat."

"You look great. I happen to like the curves."

"Curves?" The look crossing her expression sent him back a bit. "You think I'm fat?"

"Hell no." Her question sounded like something Andrea would have said. God! Were all women so touchy about their weight? He cleared his throat and looked her in the eye, his gaze conveying the truth in his next words. "Didn't you hear me? I said I like curves. You don't see me complaining when your sweet little ass is nestled in my groin, do you?" He hadn't meant to be so crude, but he'd had it with trying to console women on what he liked and didn't like. And her curvy rear end was a huge turn-on for him.

"Duly noted," she said, looking down at the paper napkin she started rolling and unrolling. Finally, she sighed. "Look, I have to be honest. I'm attracted to you. And I think you are to me too." She glanced up at him, her expression expectant. "Am I right?"

When he nodded and told her to go on, she did. "I'm not great at the sex thing."

News to him, but he didn't say so, just let her continue. "Can't we spend some time getting to know each other? So what if we end up in bed? Is making love such a bad thing when there's obviously something between us?"

That logic was the straw that broke the camel's back of his conscience. "I'd love nothing more, but first I'd like you to see where I spend a lot of my time and energies."

If he was going to get involved with her, which the jury had already convicted on that count, he at the very least had to let her see what was important to him.

They finished dessert and their wine and he stood. "I'll pick you up tomorrow around noon. Dress casually."

***

Mary Ann followed him out of the little café, wondering where he was taking her tomorrow.

The companionable silence she'd missed for a week was back between them, and her entire body was on edge because she couldn't wait for the next day. She couldn't wait to get to know him better. His plan was actually better than hers, but it also gave her time to think, and when she thought about what was going to eventually happen between them, her anticipation grew. Heavens, she hoped anticipation wouldn't eclipse the act itself, like it had in Steve's case. Yet, the more she was with Kyle, the more she knew the man beside her was nothing like Steve. Kyle Davidson would never leave her with false assumptions. He was as honest as the day was long.

Kyle pulled up next to her Camry, the only vehicle left in the studio parking lot. He killed the engine, then proceeded to help her out of the car.

The night was quiet as he opened her door and waited until she turned the key in the ignition.

He laughed along with her when, out of habit, her left foot searched for a clutch pedal that wasn't there. All humor died the instant she looked up at him and saw the blatant desire flare in his eyes. There lurked the passion Frau Haubner wanted to unleash. Same as her. When he leaned down and kissed her, his lips lingering for longer than a minute, she moaned and prayed she'd be able to handle an affair with him. Somehow she sensed once they made love, she'd never be able to forget him.

"Thanks for a great evening. I'll pick you up tomorrow at noon." He slammed her car door and walked quickly back to his Z.

Once inside, it was obvious he was waiting for her to leave. Such a nice guy, she thought, putting the car into gear and easing out of the space.

Maybe Sam was right. Maybe her gutsy moves tonight had prodded him into action. Then another thought struck. Maybe once their passion was spent, there would be nothing left. Though the very idea left her feeling bereft, Mary Ann wasn't willing to let this opportunity slide by.

What if she gained his love instead?

Chapter 11

The next day, Mary Ann rushed to open the outside door when she saw Kyle about to ring her bell. He was on time, as promised.

"Hey, gorgeous."

"Hey, gorgeous yourself." She grinned, remembering the exact exchange the first night they'd danced together. Only two weeks had passed, but it seemed like a lifetime ago.

They drove to the outskirts of Tracy. Mary Ann couldn't fathom why he was driving so far away. "What's out here besides horses and farms?"

"Wait and see," was all he said. Eventually he turned onto a winding road leading to what looked to be another farm.

He shoved the car into park and turned off the ignition. "Well, what do you think?"

Mary Ann glanced around with interest. "Looks like a farm," she stated honestly.

"It is, but not just any farm."

Too eager to wait for his assistance, Mary Ann exited the car at the same time as Kyle. Her curiosity had long killed the cat inside her. Kids' laughter drew her attention. She covered her eyes to block out the mid-November sun. The day was a beautiful sunny one, not uncommon this time of year. Although this far inland, the temperature dropped low enough in the mornings for frost. Tracy was on the northern edge of California's central valley, one of the biggest growing areas in the country.

Kyle motioned for her to walk ahead of him. "Come on and meet the kids. I have a feeling they'll love you."

When they neared the chain-link fence, she spotted more than a dozen kids playing baseball. Most were boys who looked to be middle schoolers like Kyle's brother, Brad. The few girls appeared to be slightly older, but not by much.

When one of the boys noticed them, he pointed and said something to the rest of the kids. One by one, they dropped their bat or glove or whatever they were doing and ran to the fence.

Their fingers gripping the fence, the kids' curiosity was written on their vivid faces.

"What's going on, Mr. Z?"

Kyle smiled and opened the gate. He waited for Mary Ann to step inside and then closed it.

"How's it going, Ziggy? Still hate me?"

"Nah. I kind of like it here. I get three squares a day and no one's shooting at me." Then his boastful expression turned solemn. "Is my ma okay?"

"She's fine. I told her how well you were doing, and nothing could make her happier." He gave him a pointed look. "You know all she wants is for you to do well?"

Nodding, Ziggy toed the dirt with his shoe. Then he looked up and squinted. "So, who's your lady friend?"

Chuckling, Kyle reached for her.

Feeling a little shy, Mary Ann waved once she stood in front of Kyle. "Hi. I'm Mary Ann," she said to the eight boys and three girls who'd circled around her with gazes full of interest. Lame thing to say, but anything else got stuck in her throat at the realization of what this place obviously was.

"Introduce yourselves to Mary Ann, guys," Kyle urged.

Needing no further encouragement, they each took turns stating their names and how old they were.

One by one, they trickled back to their baseball game. When the last child was out of earshot, she glanced at Kyle. "These are your kids?"

His chest actually puffed out in pride as he said, "Yeah. What do you think?"

"I don't know what to think." She glanced around the place again. "It's so crazy. I never in a million years expected this of you." If she hadn't loved him before, what she saw pushed her the rest of the way. How could she not love someone so caring? "I grew up with kids who got lost in the system." She cleared the huge lump lodged in her throat and blinked the moisture from her eyes. "The ones I remember most were about their ages."

She looked at Kyle as the image of her best friend since grade school flashed in front of her eyes, followed with the image of her slain body after a drive-by shooting, not two blocks from her house. Apparently Juanita had a drug habit, and owed money to a bunch of drug-dealing thugs who killed her because they wanted to make an example of her. Mary Ann gave Kyle an abbreviated version of her story, ending with, "That's when I realized how hard life can be for some." She brushed away an escaping tear. "We never had a lot of money, but my parents were there for me."

The look passing between her and Kyle seared her soul. He understood exactly what she'd meant. As unfathomable as that was, coming from someone with his background, she could only marvel over finding him.

***

They spent the afternoon playing softball. At the end of the game as they walked toward the main building, Kyle tugged on Mary Ann's cap. "I never realized you were so competitive."

"Me?" Her shocked expression added to the one word and he laughed. She looked out from beneath the ball cap. "I was thinking along the same lines, only you were out for blood."

"Don't take it personally. I just like to win."

"Oh, yeah," she said, exhaling an unladylike snort. "That's why Frau Haubner deserted us for Steve and Taylor? Because you like to win?"

"That was different." His gaze zeroed in on her lips. "I was fighting another battle."

Her eyebrow rose. "Oh?"

Kyle hooked an arm around her neck and pulled her to him. "Don't play coy. You knew exactly what game you were playing. I chose to win it in a different way." He then planted a kiss on her forehead and nodded at the kids who were heading for the main building. "Come on. Let's eat. Then we can go home."

"Home?"

"Yes. I'm kidnapping you and taking you to my dungeon tonight."

"I have a job and an important meeting I can't miss tomorrow."

"I'll make sure you're home in plenty of time to make it to work."

She shook her head. "I'm not a morning person. Plus, I don't like to be rushed. I need clothes and makeup and jewelry."

"That presents a problem."

"Maybe, but it's non-negotiable. You want me to spend the night, you have to drive me home and wait while I pack a bag."

"You know you are GU, don't you?" he grumbled.

"GU?"

"Geographically undesirable. You live too far south."

She laughed and looped an arm around his waist. "I may be geographically undesirable, but my other attributes more than make up for it."

"Come on, Mr. Z. You're gonna miss dinner."

Kyle turned and waved. "We're coming. Hold a spot for us, Ziggy." He shot a glance at Mary Ann. "So, what do you think about all this," he said, gesturing with his hand to indicate the entire place.

Mary Ann smiled up at him. "I think it's wonderful. What's more, I think you're wonderful."

Kyle grunted, but inside he was grinning like an idiot. "My stepmother would disagree with you." Mary Ann's approval eased some of the disappointment of always seeking it from his dad and never quite measuring up to his standards.

"Well, I'm not her."

"No, you're not." Mary Ann was the complete opposite of Stephie. That had to be why he felt comfortable around her.

During dinner Kyle kept glancing at his watch, not realizing it was noticeable until Ziggy asked, "Is something wrong, Mr. Z?"

"Hmm?" Pulled out of his thoughts, Kyle glanced up and Ziggy pointed to his watch. "You gotta be somewhere?"

He shook his head, but the meal couldn't be over fast enough for him. When his gaze landed on Mary Ann and he caught her smug smile as she took a bite of mashed potatoes, he straightened. That grin told him she understood fully why he was antsy. Yet having gone through hell and back waiting for the next stage, he had a right to be a little antsy.

Finally the bell rang, indicating dinner was over. Holly stood in the doorway. "It's time for quiet reflection. Say good-bye to Mr. Davidson and his friend." She turned to them and said, "Unless you'd prefer to stay."

Ordinarily Kyle would like nothing better, but not tonight. "Thanks, but we have to get back." Of course, he didn't like admitting that spending time with Mary Ann trumped staying longer. The kids would be fine. He'd spent the afternoon with them and they knew he'd be back again. Besides, quiet reflection was something personal for these kids. It was better if he didn't attend. They each needed to find spirituality in their own way, give themselves to a higher power, like alcoholics did to overcome their problems. Faith kept them moving forward, as did hope.

***

Kyle wended his way out the same road they'd driven in on.

"What a great place," Mary Ann said, gazing out the window. "How did you ever find it?"

"I didn't find it. I created it."

Her head snapped up and he now had Mary Ann's full attention. He glanced over to see her mouth gaped open. Tipping her chin to close it, he said, "You're collecting flies."

Immediately her mouth clamped shut, but only for a moment. "You created it?" Awe filled her voice. "As in, built it?"

"Yeah," he admitted, sighing. "Now you know why I'm not such a great catch. The few women I've had relationships with don't understand my need to spend so much time out here."

Mary Ann waved her hand dismissively. "Those women are fools."

A flush of pleasure rode up his spine, even as the conviction in her voice tugged on something deep inside of him. His heart. He'd often wondered if he even had one. True, he cared for Grams. And his brother. And his kids. They were easy to care for because their need never stretched his desire to give. Something told him Mary Ann would stretch that ability, and he honest to God didn't know if he had it in him to give her what she'd most likely demand at some point.

At the I-580/I-680 split he headed south, and eventually veered off the interstate. He guided the Z to a vacant spot right in front of her building.

"I won't be long," she said.

While she was gone, Kyle's conscience began pecking away again. In response, he threw back a few rational arguments. She was a big girl, as she'd pointed out too many times. He wasn't doing anything she didn't want. She knew the rules.

Yes, but can you live with hurting her? And there was the hundred dollar question.

As Mary Ann rushed toward him, a huge wave of doubt rolled over him. His expression must have given his thoughts away because the moment she'd belted herself inside the car, she turned to him and said, "Okay, out with it."

"What?"

"You're not having second thoughts about tonight, are you?"

"No," he lied, pushing the START button on the car. He

disengaged the clutch and shifted into first gear. The car responded and soon they were back on the interstate heading north.

The point of no return, he thought. He glanced at Mary Ann.

As if sensing his attention, she turned and bestowed on him one of her bright smiles. Immediately, his doubts lessened. He inhaled a deep breath, praying he wouldn't disappoint her like his dad had disappointed him.

Eventually, he exited the freeway and wound his way toward the water's edge. He pulled into a driveway and pressed the garage door opener located at the bottom of his rearview mirror.

Within minutes, he was shoving the freight elevator gate up. After placing his hand on the small of her back, he guided her inside his spacious home that was really a warehouse he'd converted ten years ago.

She shoved her hands in her pockets as he gave her a tour, which basically amounted to pointing and explaining the different sections of his condo that took up an entire floor, with a view of San Francisco Bay on one side and Lake Merritt on the other. "This was one of my first projects."

"Impressive." She did a three-sixty as he went to turn on the gas fireplace. "You did all this?"

The blaze ignited and he stood to face her. "Yes. Do you like it?"

"What's not to like?" She walked the length of the space, peering around the screens he used as walls. "It's absolutely beautiful."

Relaxing his shoulders, he exhaled the breath he hadn't known he was holding in. "I'm glad you like my taste."

"I still can't get over the fact that you did all of this yourself."

Feeling ten feet tall, he threw his shoulders back. "I had help." He then went on to explain how he'd started his small construction company. "All I did was hire the right men. They're the ones who actually did most of the work." He paused to gauge her reaction. "From there the company grew, and was ten times bigger when my dad bought me out."

Mary Ann made her way to stand in front of one of his two huge picture windows, then glanced back at him. "Your dad bought you out?"

"Yeah. He made me an offer I couldn't refuse when the economy tanked a few years ago." Kyle hadn't regretted his move. "So now I work for him."

"Wow. I didn't expect that."

He smiled ruefully. "Neither did I. But back then, too many people depended on me and my company's solvency for their livelihood." Now those same workers owed their livelihood to his dad, who'd assured him as long as Kyle's employees worked to their same standards, they'd always have a job. It was the only reason Kyle had signed on the dotted line.

"Would you like a glass of wine?" he asked to change the subject.

"Sure." She rubbed her arms but kept her gaze fastened on the view outside as he busied himself at the bar pouring two glasses.

After picking up both, he strode up to her. "Cold?"

She shook her head as she took the glass of wine he offered.

He brought his glass to his lips and studied her. If she wasn't cold, she was nervous. So am I, he thought, wiping sweaty palms on his jeans. Hell, he didn't remember being this nervous the first time he ever made love. To Jen, his high school sweetheart. They were together two years until she left for college. Jen was the first to tell him he wasn't husband material.

"It's romantic," Mary Ann said before taking a sip. "The lights of San Francisco in the background and the new Bay Bridge lit up like it is. If I had this place, I'd never want to leave."

"The views are why I bought the building, which was a dump and needed a lot of work." Would Mary Ann think the same way as Jen? At the time, he'd thought they'd marry. But look how that turned out.

She turned to face him. With her glass near her lips, she smiled. "You're a surprising man, Mr. Z." She then set her glass down and reached for his.

When he relinquished his hold on the stem, he watched in stunned fascination as her smile turned seductive. He couldn't stop his hands from touching her hair. For too long, he'd wondered what it felt like. Soft and full, like tiny strands of fluff. He picked up a handful and brought it to his face, smelling the faint scent of lavender. He recognized the scent because his mother always burned lavender candles when she was alive.

The thought sent a searing pain to his heart. What if he loved her and lost her too? Could he handle the loss? He wasn't entirely sure. The thought dissipated when she reached up on her toes and kissed him. Need, want, and desire crashed together in one huge wave, swamping him with a craving he'd never felt before.

He guided her to the rug in front of the fireplace. The blaze felt warm on his back as he lowered her to the floor. One by one, each piece of clothing was discarded until they were both naked in front of the blazing hearth.

She shivered.

"Are you cold?"

"No, just happy to finally be here with you. Like this."

Kyle lowered his mouth and when their lips connected, it was as if he'd come in from the cold after a long winter's night. Mary Ann was everything he'd ever wanted and more.

Chapter 12

Sunshine beamed through the open blinds in the window, warming Mary Ann's face. Squinting at the bright light shining right on her, she sat up. The top sheet dropped below her naked breasts. It took her a moment to remember where she was.

Stretching, she turned to see Kyle still sleeping soundly. He looked so peaceful. So endearing with his mouth open. A flush of heat rose up her face at the thought of how much pleasure that mouth had brought forth with a few well-placed strokes. The man certainly knew how to please a woman. But would it last?

She had no more time to obsess over the thought because Kyle opened one eye and groaned. "Are you staring at me?" He stretched.

"No." She glanced away, then laughed at how silly she must seem. "I mean yes." Her gaze traveled back to his well-defined chest. "You have to admit, you present a very pleasant picture."

"Pleasant?" He squinted. "First I'm nice, then I'm pretentious, and now I'm pleasant?" His sigh came out in one audible huff. "I expected more after giving you three orgasms. Apparently my sexual prowess had no effect on you."

"Of course it did, but I was being polite because you sleep with your mouth open."

"I do not."

"Yes, you do and it's adorable."

"Now I'm adorable." He plopped his head back on the pillow and rubbed a hand over his face. "God, I'll never live this down."

Mary Ann was about to say more, but spotted the clock on the nightstand. "Oh my God! I'm late. I should have been at work an hour ago."

"It's only five after eight." He reached for her thigh and trailed a finger down the outside length of it. "You can always call in sick."

"Not today I can't. I have a big presentation to make." She grabbed her things and hurried toward his bathroom, the only enclosed space on the entire floor. "You need to get dressed too. I'll need a ride to BART."

"You're not taking BART. I'll drive you to your office." He stumbled out of bed and stretched some more.

"That's not necessary." She glanced briefly over her shoulders and couldn't help but notice he was naked. "Put some clothes on. You're distracting me."

Laughing, Kyle reached for his boxers that were really long briefs. After putting them on, he then stepped into his jeans.

As she turned on the shower, he shouted, "I'll make the coffee and then I'll drive you to Hayward."

Despite all her arguments against it, Kyle wouldn't hear of dropping her off at the station.

When he pulled up in front of her office building forty-five minutes later, she watched as he hurried around to her door, opened it, and held out a helping hand.

Now out of the car, Mary Ann turned back to him, wondering when she'd see him again.

As if her thoughts were plastered on her face, he leaned in to kiss her. "I'll call you sometime today to arrange our next practice session." He then turned and climbed into his car as quickly as he'd climbed out of it.

Mary Ann stood staring at the Z's retreat. She spun around to enter her building only when his taillights were out of her line of vision.

Already she missed him.

***

The next three weeks flew by. Glorious weeks that, outside of work, were spent together. They practiced dancing every night. By now, Mary Ann was staying at Kyle's warehouse loft so they could practice. Their relationship fell into a routine. He'd pick her up at BART, they'd have a romantic dinner in some fancy restaurant Kyle knew, or he'd cook for her. A man of many talents, Kyle was first and foremost a gourmet cook.

Tonight, he was working late, which had left her time for checking out her apartment, doing laundry, and collecting a few necessary things.

"Kyle," she shouted upon her return, having let herself in with the spare key he'd given her. The loft was empty so she set about making him dinner. Her cooking skills weren't up to his level, but she could whip up a decent casserole to pop in the oven. That way it would stay warm until Kyle made it home.

Home. She looked around and wondered if this would ever be her home. Kyle had yet to mention anything about long-term, and she didn't want to jinx it by becoming demanding. Geez, they'd only known each other a little over a month. But what a wonderful, romantic month it had been.

Several hours later, Mary Ann pulled the casserole out of the oven.

She glanced at the door, then at her watch. Ten thirty. Where was he? Rolling the kinks out of her shoulders, she went to stand in front of the huge window facing the bay. Before when she'd looked out it was romantic, but now it was lonely. Mainly because she felt lonely. She checked her phone. No texts or calls from Kyle. After another half hour of pacing, she switched on the gas fireplace and made herself comfortable on the sofa.

The next thing she knew, Kyle was kissing her awake, having knelt in front of her while she slept.

Blinking, she sat up and looked around. "I must have dozed off." Her gaze landed on the granite kitchen counter. "I cooked dinner, but it's overdone. I thought you'd be here earlier."

"I'm sorry. I got wrapped up in something at work. This morning a kid went missing at the farm, which compounded the problem at work because I couldn't be two places at once."

"You know how to use a cell phone, don't you?" She hadn't meant to sound cryptic.

His answer was just as cryptic. "Yes. I'm well aware of phone etiquette, but when I'm out pouring concrete in the rain, I leave it in my truck. Besides, I thought you had things to take care of at your apartment."

"I did, but I decided to surprise you with dinner." She tried for a smile, but it fell short. "I guess the surprise was on me."

Sighing, he sat down next to her. "It's been one hell of a day."

"Want to tell me about it?"

He shook his head. "I want to forget it ever happened." He stood and headed for the bathroom. "I need a hot shower."

Having never seen this uncommunicative, surly side of Kyle, Mary Ann didn't know what to do. Had she overstepped her bounds by assuming he wanted her here? His manner was too much like Steve's, right before he told her he needed space. Was this the beginning of the end? Mary Ann wasn't going to wait around to find out, only to endure a repeat performance. As the sound of running water came from the other room, she quickly gathered her things and tiptoed out the door, locking it behind her.

A few tears escaped her eyes, and she brushed them away as she made her way to the freeway entrance.

On the Nimitz, she floored the gas pedal. If only she could make it home, she'd be okay.

***

Rubbing his head with a towel, Kyle said while heading for the bedroom, "You coming to bed?" Too beat to wait for an answer, much less have to explain himself, he climbed into bed and was asleep within seconds of his head hitting the pillow.

The next morning, he groggily rolled over and reached for Mary Ann. His hand hit an empty space. Kyle sat up and shook off sleep. Where in the hell was she? Panicked at the thought that she'd left, he jumped out of bed.

"Mary Ann?" he called out half a dozen times while checking each and every cranny in the spacious loft. He slid the shower curtain closed as realization set in. She had indeed left him. The panic spread to his heart, and a pain of loss he hadn't felt since he first made love with her filled him with more panic.

He grabbed his cell phone and sent her a text. *Where are you?*

Working, popped up seconds later. The response calmed his nerves and seemed reasonable. He glanced at the clock. Of course she was at work. Where else would she be at eight thirty? Still, as he moved around his loft, the feeling of dread—of somehow screwing things up—wouldn't leave him.

Are we practicing tonight? Kyle typed hours later after not hearing from Mary Ann.

Where?

At my place. Where else?

What time?

Was she crazy or was she putting him through this to make a point? *The usual time. I should be done early today. Tragedies only happen on Mondays,* he typed to be funny.

Are you sure you want me there?

He shook his head and muttered, "Women." *Yes, I'm sure.* And just to mess with her, he typed, *Are you sure you want to come?*

What does that mean?

Beats me. I hope I see you tonight at the BART station.

Kyle didn't get a response and wasn't a hundred percent sure she'd make it.

For the rest of what was left of the day, he obsessed about Mary Ann.

Would she or wouldn't she? It was enough to make a guy crazy. I don't need this shit, he thought, combing a hand through his hair and rubbing his neck. Kyle was quickly learning he wasn't a patient person where Mary Ann was concerned. He loved her.

The hand massaging his neck stopped and his heartbeat quickened. Christ, where had that thought come from?

No. He didn't love her. The very notion scared him shitless. He wouldn't allow himself to love her. Because that meant he'd eventually lose her.

Twenty minutes before her train was supposed to make the station, Kyle broke down and called her. "Hey, gorgeous," he said after she answered.

"Hey, gorgeous yourself." Her reply had him exhaling a sigh of relief. She sounded normal. "I wanted to make sure you were on the train."

Her laughter shot from the small device to his ears, zinging all the way to his groin. Maybe he did love her after all, and maybe it didn't mean he'd lose her. Tonight he would tell her what he was thinking.

He kept waiting for the right moment to open up to her as they practiced, but that moment never came. Mary Ann was her bright and bubbly self, but some wariness in her expression kept him from blurting out what was in his heart. What if she didn't feel the same?

When it was time to start cooking dinner, he decided to wait and see what the next week brought. Why risk rejection when it was too soon in the relationship to be spouting off about love and commitment in the first place?

After adding water to the pot, he put the pan on the stove top, and flipped on the burner. He turned to lean against the counter and crossed his arms. "So, what happened last night?" His eyebrows rose as he glanced at her.

Mary Ann's expression hardened a bit. "I was going to ask you the same thing."

"I asked first." He smiled, but the pain lodged in his throat kept it from reaching his eyes. "Why did you leave?"

She shrugged. "Why would I stay? It was obvious you wanted

to be alone."

His jaw dropped open. Her statement floored him. He was about to deny it, but stopped to think about her claim. "I wasn't in the mood for company last night," he finally admitted. "The morning was bad enough." He explained about one of his kids, whose drug-addicted father had stormed the facility wanting to pick up the boy. "Holly had to deal with him until law enforcement arrived, which was only minutes before I got there." He counted to ten to still the urge to hit something. Situations where the kid took the brunt of both societal and parental pitfalls frustrated him no end.

"Then I had some major problems at work to undo," he added when he could talk without showing any of his inner turmoil. "One of the workers almost died because he didn't know what he was doing. By the time Fred figured it out, a fourth of the job had been done. We had to tear it out and begin again."

"How horrible."

"Yeah, and more horrible when I had to fire the guy." He sighed and rubbed his temples to ease the headache he felt coming on just thinking about yesterday. "He came highly recommended, but he was useless. I can deal with useless. Stupid gets people killed." The joker, who was both, hadn't mixed the cement to code, thinking he was saving the company money. A lawsuit twenty years from now didn't bother him, since he'd be long gone. But Kyle would still be here. And worse, others could die if the building collapsed due to cutting corners. "I'm sorry I was such an ass. I had a lot on my mind."

Kyle peered directly into her eyes. "Are we okay now?"

"Sure." Nodding, Mary Ann smiled, but only halfheartedly. Hurt, disillusionment, or sadness—he wasn't sure which—lurked in her expression.

Afraid to push, he held out his arms and was somewhat relieved when she didn't hesitate to step into them.

Chapter 13

"Let's practice that turn again," Mary Ann said, drawing Kyle's attention. "I don't want to miss my count and step on your foot during our performance. Otherwise, Frau Haubner may have a coronary."

Kyle nodded and the two got into hold. "Ready?" he asked. The turn she was talking about was a waltz turn, and Kyle would gladly practice it because it meant holding her in his arms, something he'd never pass up. He enjoyed ballroom dancing—enjoyed the power of leading his partner around the room—more than he thought possible. When the music flowed through him as Frau Haubner had instructed him to allow, he loved the sensation of floating around the room with Mary Ann in his arms. He'd die before he'd let anyone in on that secret, though.

They did the maneuver three times perfectly before Mary Ann was satisfied.

By this time the eight other couples, including the Hendersons, gathered at the front of the stage for today's lesson.

"Tonight is our final night together." Frau Haubner's gaze swept each student individually as she spoke. "You have all learned three difficult dances. I will allow the first hour for practice and will be available to help perfect the steps." Smiling, she inclined her head. "Then, the competition will begin."

The hour passed quickly as everyone vied for Frau Haubner's attention.

She broke away from the couple she'd been helping and clapped. "We will begin the competition with Kyle Davidson and his partner, Mary Ann Murphy, doing the waltz."

"This is going to be fun," Kyle said after the dragon lady next introduced the judges, three instructors who taught at the studio on different nights.

"Yes." Mary Ann shook her hands and shifted her weight from foot to foot. "It will be exactly like the show."

"Don't be nervous," he said, reaching for her hand and

squeezing.

"I can't help it. I have a thousand butterflies flapping inside my tummy."

"Relax. It's just a dance," he whispered, placing his other hand on her back and lifting their joined hands to shoulder height to start in hold position. He smiled down at her and winked. "Do it like we practiced and forget about everyone in the room but me."

The music started and Kyle knew if he could lead her, she'd follow. Dancing wasn't just the steps. It was the intricate balance between feeling the melody and letting it guide you through the movement.

He expunged every thought but the feel of Mary Ann in his arms. The music surrounded them as he gracefully glided through the different moves they'd practiced since the dragon lady had taught them weeks ago. As he looked down and she looked up at the same time, they became one. Gazes locked, he finished their dance with the turn they'd just gotten through practicing.

Frau Haubner clapped, a pleased smile crossing her face. "Precisely how a waltz should be danced. You took my breath away."

Kyle ignored the other students' applause, having eyes only for Mary Ann.

A hint of pink colored her cheeks. She stepped back and cleared her throat as Kyle continued staring at her. Had she felt the magic too?

She offered a shy smile and finally meeting his gaze, she shrugged. "That was wonderful. Thank you."

Feeling somewhat off-kilter, Kyle returned a wobbly smile. "You're welcome." He leaned in and his smile widened. "I think we showed the Hendersons how it's done."

Her gurgle of laughter erupted. The sound sent a jolt to his groin, and he had to remind himself they were in public. He couldn't wait to get her alone. A glance at the clock had him groaning. Another fifty-five minutes to go.

"I'll be right back," Mary Ann said. "I need to go to the powder room."

When she was out of sight, Kyle felt a sense of loneliness he didn't understand. Worse, his chest tightened and fear gripped him. Several deep breaths helped calm him, as did the shoulder lifts to relieve the tension in his spine. He had nothing to fear, he decided, pushing away the silly notion something ominous was about to happen.

**

Mary Ann made her way to the sink and spotted Taylor Henderson. Taylor must have followed her into the ladies' room. The next stall over was still vacant. Even more interesting, the woman appeared to be waiting for someone, continuing to stand near the door the entire time she washed her hands.

"I know your kind," Taylor said in a vicious tone when she turned off the water.

Deciding to pay no attention to her, Mary Ann reached for a paper towel.

"Don't ignore me." She leaned in closer and practically hissed, "You think Kyle Davidson of Davidson Construction is interested in you?" Her features twisted in disgust. "Think again."

She couldn't believe the woman could be so bold. "It's really none of your business," Mary Ann said, making eye contact. It was no big secret that his family had money.

"He's one of the most sought-after bachelors in the Bay Area, but his relationships don't last."

"Your point?"

"You're a nobody. Once he gets what he wants from you, he'll drop you. Just like Steve did."

"Steve isn't fit to wipe Kyle's boots."

Some of Mary Ann's inner turmoil must have shown in her eyes, because Taylor's lips curled into a semblance of a smile. "Oh my God. You're in love with him. That's rich," she said, practically cackling. "Even if Kyle's MO with women changed and you managed to rein him in, I know his mother. She'd never allow someone like you into her family."

Everything inside her being was shaking, but she kept it together, refusing to let the woman get to her. "I've met Stephie Davidson." Mirroring the woman's cruel smile, Mary Ann shook her head. "You're wrong. On two counts. One, she's his stepmother, not his mother. Two, I doubt she has any sway over Kyle's choice of a partner." Still shaking, Mary Ann finished drying her hands and tossed the towel in the trash using perfect aim. "What's the matter, Taylor?" she said, looking her square in the eyes. "Not happy with stealing Steve, you want to take Kyle too?" She shook her head. "There's a name for women like you, but I'm too polite to use it." Then, holding her head high, she strode swiftly out of the room, pausing only long enough to open the door.

Outside the restroom, she realized her hands still shook. Unwilling to let Kyle see her like this, she headed for the exit as her cell phone rang.

"Hi, Mom," she said when she answered it, thankful for her call. If anyone could cheer her up, it was Colleen Murphy, a rock Mary Ann had recently discovered.

"Hi, sweetie. How're the dance lessons going?"

Fine." She grinned as the last few minutes faded. "I think Kyle and I have a good chance at winning our competition."

"How wonderful. Sam told me you two are officially dating. I knew that boy was the one for you the minute Maggie told me he agreed to our plan."

"Plan?" Her heartbeat sped up and her ears grew hot even as a cold sensation ran down her spine. "Kyle was part of your plan?"

"Well, yes and no. He agreed to take you out. As for the dance lessons, we had the bingo committee's help."

"Are you serious?" When Mary Ann realized she had a death grip on the phone, she switched hands. Kyle agreed to take her out before she won the lessons? "Are you telling me he knew all along about your scheme?"

"Of course he knew. But it doesn't matter. The end result is what really counts. So, when is the wedding?"

"Oh, for heaven's sake, Mom. Kyle hasn't even told me he loves me."

"But you love him, right? Sam told me so."

Oh God, this was going from bad to worse. "Look, Mom, when I have news about any plans, you'll be the first to know."

"Don't wait too long to make your way to the altar. You're not getting any younger, and those eggs won't keep forever."

"Now you sound like Maggie." She rolled her eyes and counted to ten to keep the tears from falling.

"Well, it's true."

"I gotta go, Mom. I'm right in the middle of our last class. I'll call you later."

"Okay. Maggie and Irma send their love. Say hi to Kyle for us."

"Will do." Mary Ann ended the conversation, then blinked to clear her vision as doubt a mile wide cut her in two. Were the last six weeks due to Kyle, the proverbial nice guy, being nice? Lord, she hoped not.

Yet Taylor's voice kept playing over and over in her brain—a DVD that wouldn't shut off, and one that didn't make her feel any better.

He'll never marry you.

It took a few more minutes to pull herself together before she could walk back into the room.

One of the couples was doing a decent cha-cha as Kyle glanced her way, his eyebrows lifting in question.

She shrugged in answer and slowly made her way to him. He'd never mentioned love and she'd never asked for it. No, instead she'd thrown herself at him and expected love in return. Maybe that had worked for Sam, but it didn't seem to be working for her.

"Are you okay? I saw Taylor go into the ladies' room and when she came out, she didn't look happy."

"I put her in her place, is all."

Kyle smiled, the one that always did strange things to her insides. Maybe he did love her. She'd come this far; why not go for the gold, as Sam would say. "But I'm not going to conk him over the head," she muttered under her breath.

"What?" Kyle asked, looking at her strangely. "Are you sure you're okay?"

With a frozen smile pasted on her face, she said, "Of course. Why wouldn't I be?"

He leaned in and whispered, "Don't forget, tomorrow night you promised you'd go with me to my stepmother's birthday dinner."

"I haven't forgotten." She swallowed the excuse on the tip of her tongue when she caught his pleading stare. "I have it marked in big letters on my calendar."

"You're spending the night with me, but I can drop you off tomorrow to pick a formal dress." Then as if not sure, he threw her a worried look. "You have one, don't you?"

"Yes. I have one." She pursed her lips to keep from adding, *And I know how to act at a formal affair, contrary to others' opinions.*

"Good." He turned back to the couple on the dance floor, unaware she was seething inside. Whether from hurt, annoyance, or plain unhappiness, she didn't know. Breathe, she told herself. Just breathe and don't listen to anyone who says you're not worthy. Those words had become her mantra after Steve's rejection. Funny how she gave it credence now, when in reality this was a totally different situation. She only had to remember Kyle had done nothing wrong. True, he hadn't told her he loved her yet, but could she really expect it so early in their relationship?

The couple ended their cha-cha and Mary Ann applauded along with the rest of the class.

She managed to survive the next forty minutes, but most of it was spent obsessing about Taylor's comments and her mother's phone call. Both replayed in her mind so many times, the rejected part of Mary Ann tried to convince the logical side that Kyle could never love her. To the point that when the last couple left the dance floor, Mary Ann prayed she and Kyle wouldn't win.

How could she endure six more weeks, if the man she loved viewed her as a charity case, much like his kids? How had she not seen the similarities?

On the other hand, what if that was all it was? Similarities? How could she just give up after that last dance?

"The winners of the Oakland Park Dance competition, earning the couple six more ballroom dancing lessons by unanimous vote, are—" The announcement broke into her thoughts. Mary Ann glanced toward the stage and held her breath as the room went silent.

The announcer dragged it out, like on TV. Couldn't he just get on with it?

"Kyle Davidson and his partner, Mary Ann Murphy."

Oh God! Mary Ann clamped a hand over her mouth to hide her shock. They won? They actually won. As Kyle swept her into a bear hug, lifting her off her feet and twirling her around, her insecurities faded. Taylor was wrong, she thought, seeing the joy in his eyes when he set her down. So what if he'd gone along with the setup? He was here now, and the look passing between them did much to assuage the naysayer inside her.

"Think you can handle six more weeks?" Kyle asked, his heated gaze telling her he was willing and able.

Her grin spread. "I can if you can." Of course he was a nice guy, a complete opposite of Steve. Kyle was also the man she fell in love with. So what if he was in on her mom and Maggie's scheme from the beginning? After all, Mary Ann wouldn't even have gone out with him if she'd known. He might not love her yet, but she felt certain he was heading in that direction.

Now was not the time to back down or demand explanations. Tonight was for celebrating.

Chapter 14

The champagne cork popped and the small missile hit the high ceiling. Kyle poured two glasses and handed one to Mary Ann.

"To the most beautiful dancer in the world." Holding on to his solemn expression, he locked gazes with her. "You were fabulous tonight."

"I'll drink to that."

He took a drink and sighed, his satisfied smile sneaking out. "Damn, it felt good to beat them."

"Yeah." She looked at him with raised eyebrows. "So, where do we go from here?"

Something in her eyes stopped him from saying what was in his heart—that he wanted her with him always. What if she wasn't on the same page? Or worse, what if she was upset about six more lessons? Kyle dismissed those thoughts as ridiculous, especially the last one, but the first still lurked in the background of his mind, waiting. For now, he'd follow Mary Ann's lead.

With that idea in mind, he studied her as she studied him. Finally, she broke eye contact and lifted her champagne flute.

After taking a sip, she cupped a hand over her mouth, clearly stifling a giggle. "This champagne is delicious, but the bubbles tickle my nose."

He set his glass on the counter. The movement drew her attention to his hand and then her stare moved higher. Smiling warmly, he flipped on the sound system's CD player and the room filled with a waltz he'd recorded earlier. Then he beckoned with his hand. "Come here."

The question was back in her eyes. "What?"

"I'll show you where we go from here." He decided to use his body to tell her how he felt. In turn, he'd listen to what her body told him.

Like earlier that evening he led her in a graceful waltz, but unlike the previous dance, this time they didn't have an audience. Swaying to the beat, he kept his gaze fastened on hers. Every now and then her thigh would brush his full erection and the contact only made him harder.

The practiced steps came easily. The turns and dips he led her through were a prelude to their lovemaking. As the music faded, he slowed his steps. When he could do so gracefully, he bent his head. Putting all the love in his heart into the kiss, he lowered his mouth and connected with hers. His lips lingered, drinking in anything she gave back.

In slow motion, he picked her up and carried her to the bedroom part of his loft, before gently placing her on the bed. Keeping to his slow rhythm, he undressed her, making sure he touched each part of her body in a loving way. When she was half-naked, she took control, pushing him back on the bed and unhurriedly unbuttoning his shirt.

She shoved it off his shoulders and her lips grazed where cloth once covered. In the same leisurely fashion, the rest of their clothing came off, one article at a time, one touch at a time. When he tossed her panties behind him, the last piece standing between them, he stretched out, subduing the need to plunge inside and let her warmth surround him.

Her low moans made waiting all but impossible. When she became more insistent, he stilled her hands and held them above her head while his mouth had its fill of her body. She had a lush figure made for loving.

"Do you know how lovely you are?"

Her answer was a sexy smile accompanied with a half-lidded stare that did nothing to cool his ardor.

"I want you." It was a statement of need.

"You have me," she said, her gaze softening.

"I want all of you," he whispered, taking her in his mouth. As he brought her to the cusp of completion, he felt every shudder, every moan. When at last she reached the sky, he realized his wait was over. Quickly, while she was still floating back to earth, he entered her in one fluid motion.

Her soft moans filled the air and she wrapped her arms around him, as if to bring him closer. But Kyle resisted, staying on his elbows and leaning above her.

"Mary Ann," he said, slowly stroking in and out with his lower body. "Look at me." He gritted his teeth to endure the pleasure the strokes created.

Finally, she did as he'd asked and opened her eyes.

Holding on to her gaze, he continued his slow pace. When he

felt her contractions build, he pumped faster. All too soon she climaxed, pulling him with her, and still he held fast to her gaze as pleasure so intense burst from his heart. Only when he glimpsed the same from her did he close his eyes and collapse on top of her.

"That was wonderful," she said, opening her eyes when he lifted back up on his elbows.

I love you. The three little words stuck in the back of Kyle's throat. He wanted to say them, but they wouldn't come.

Instead, he propped some pillows behind him and brought Mary Ann into his arms, holding her tightly, as if he might lose her if he didn't. He ran his hand through her hair. The shiny softness was blanketed around her shoulders. Catching a curl in between his finger and thumb, he rubbed. "I love your hair."

"Hmmm."

Kyle looked down at her beautiful face and his breath hitched. Her eyes were closed and she wore such a peace-filled expression that warmth encompassed him. He rested his head among the pillows and exhaled a contented sigh.

Things would work out as they should.

***

Mary Ann woke up to the sound of the shower running. The night before came back in a rush of memories and her satisfied smile broke free. She hugged herself as a thrill of excitement rose up her spine. In the light of day, her worries seemed senseless. Soon Kyle would tell her he loved her and once they were married, Taylor Henderson would have to eat crow.

Everything was perfect.

Except for the weather! Her gaze landed on the windows, and all she could see was mood-killing gray. Outside, the rain poured. The dreariness affected her in the opposite way the sunshine usually did. Ignoring the gloom and doom sensation engulfing her, she climbed out of bed and padded toward the kitchen area to make a cup of coffee. There was absolutely no reason to feel down. Not after such a great evening.

The bathroom door opened. With only a towel wrapped around his middle, Kyle entered the kitchen area as the coffee finished brewing.

"A woman after my own heart."

She smiled. "I aim to please."

The heated glance he shot her before he moved to pour himself a cup could incinerate bones, it was so hot. "As I found out last night," he said, leaning against the counter and crossing his legs. He took a sip, then closed his eyes and practically groaned in ecstasy. "Damn, that hits the spot after too much champagne."

"You know what they say about overindulgence?"

Raising his eyebrows, he grinned. "What?"

"It loses its effectiveness if you do it too much."

Still wearing a spine-tingling grin, he started in her direction, not stopping until he had her backed up against the breakfast bar counter. Locking stares, he hooked an arm around her neck and brought her closer. He lowered his head until his mouth was an inch from hers. "Making love with you will never lose its impact."

His breath, like a soft kiss, sent tingles through her system, and when their lips joined, it was all she could do to keep from melting.

The towel dropped. Kyle stood in front of her like a seasoned warrior ready for battle...ready to conquer her.

She tried not to blush. Making love by firelight was one thing when the world outside was dark, but in daylight, even dreary daylight, it was another thing entirely.

Mary Ann felt his soft chuckle when his chest rumbled in amusement. He leaned away and caught her gaze. "You're not shy, are you?" His head lowered to her throat, where his lips worked their way across her neck to her ear. He spent an inordinate amount of time on her lobe before whispering, "After last night, there shouldn't be any barriers between us."

Her head dropped back to give him more access as she murmured an inaudible agreement.

A heartbeat later, he was carrying her to the bed. In quick succession, her robe and slippers were discarded. She now lay naked on the bed and the moment he entered her, she wanted to shout out her love. Instead she kept her feelings inside, waiting for him to say it first.

Yet all thoughts dissipated as pleasure and fullness took their place.

Their lovemaking was slow and leisurely this morning. After another earth-shattering climax, Mary Ann stretched, feeling quite replete and unwilling to rise as Kyle moved to stand.

"We need to get moving," he said, playfully swatting her butt. "I promised the kids I'd be there before noon."

"Killjoy," she said under her breath as she jumped out of bed for the second time that morning. As she grabbed her coffee and headed toward the bathroom, she said a little louder, "Today would have been a perfect day to stay in bed."

"I'll make it up to you tomorrow," he shouted back as she shut the door.

With wet towel in hand, Mary Ann came out of the bathroom and glanced at Kyle.

"I'll be back from the farm in plenty of time to pick you up," he said, tucking in his shirt. He snapped his jeans closed. "You can still tag along. The kids love you."

Mary Ann's amused laugh rang out. "I love them too," she said, walking up to him and wrapping her arms around his waist. She leaned back and met his curious gaze. "But I need some time to myself."

"I'll miss you." Kyle lowered his head. After a quick kiss, he gave her butt another gentle swat. "Get dressed. Otherwise, I'll overindulge."

Chuckling, she shook her head. "We wouldn't want that." Then she did as he asked because she knew he was in a hurry.

***

Mary Ann took her time dressing. The short, Caribbean-blue cocktail gown—her one big splurge after her breakup with Steve— had cost a week's pay. This was the first time she actually had somewhere fancy to wear her feel-good purchase. She stepped into the shimmering sheath and wiggled as it slid over her ample hips. After struggling to pull up the zipper in the back, she straightened. Her gaze drifted to the mirror.

Satisfied, she smiled. After adding a touch more makeup, Mary Ann slipped on a few of her best pieces of jewelry. Both helped finish the look.

Nervous energy filled her as she paced. When her buzzer finally chimed, she pressed the intercom button and said, "I'll be right down." She grabbed her wrap, locked the door behind her, and practically took the stairs two at a time—not an easy feat in strappy heels.

Out on the street, Kyle whistled. "Wow, you look great." He gestured for her to turn around with his hand and she did.

"Like it?" She felt like a glow stick as he took her shawl and wrapped it around her shoulders.

"Like it? I love it." Still holding the two ends in his hands, he leaned in and kissed her forehead. "I'll have to take you out more often."

"We've been out plenty of times."

"Yes, but those are casual dates. It's nice to dress up now and then."

That was when she noticed his expertly cut suit, an expensive one, similar to those her older brother bought. Mainly because he wanted to fit in as a stockbroker. Kyle didn't appear to look like he wore the suit to impress anyone. In fact, in this case the man fit the suit, not the other way around.

When Kyle turned onto Piedmont Avenue and pulled up in front of Commis, an exclusive restaurant, Mary Ann tried to hide her trepidation. Though her brother Kevin was used to these kinds of restaurants, she'd never actually eaten in one, even when she and Steve dated. Back then, Steve was still a rising star and they usually went Dutch on evenings out. Neither could afford a two-hundred-dollar-per-person dinner. In fact, Mary Ann usually thought it pretentious to charge that much, after hearing someone complain about the food not tasting much different than places charging a quarter of the price. It was as if they were trying to keep people like her out with those high prices.

She cleared her throat, and pushed back strands of hair that had come out of the clip she wore. One she'd designed. "It seems kind of extravagant. Are you sure I'm invited?"

Kyle looked at her like she was from a different planet. "You're my date. Of course you're invited."

Allowing the valet to help her out of the car, she turned and glanced at the imposing place, feeling like a sunflower in a bouquet of roses. She stepped on the curb and waited for Kyle to finish handing over his key. "Take care of her," he said as the valet jumped inside and revved the motor.

"He looks like he can drive a stick," she said when he seemed put out as the car shot forward into traffic.

"There had better not be any scratches on it."

She laughed and grabbed his hand, whether to offer moral support or to gain it, she wasn't sure. The one thing she was certain of was that she was clearly out of her realm.

As they neared the table, Ronald stood. The hand he held out indicated his wife. "You've met Stephie?"

Mary Ann nodded. "The birthday girl, right?"

"It's impolite to remind one about getting older," she said, practically glaring at her.

Kyle leaned in. "I should have warned you. She hates to be reminded that she's like the rest of us who age a year at a time."

Then why have a birthday celebration? Without voicing the question, she sat in the chair Kyle pulled out.

During dinner, Mary Ann nervously drank the offered wine, not really paying attention to the fact that her glass rarely emptied until she began feeling tipsy. That's when she noticed the waiter discreetly refilling each glass whenever the contents reached a certain level.

She glanced around and caught Stephie staring at her like she was some kind of pariah, exactly as she'd done several times in the past half hour. No wonder she was guzzling the wine.

"I see your friend is thirsty." Stephie offered a brittle smile. "Maybe we should get her her own bottle."

Mary Ann swallowed hard and threw Kyle an apologetic glance. "I'm just a little nervous," she admitted.

Ronald smiled indulgently. "Eating with us can make anyone nervous." He spoke in a joking manner, but something in his eyes kept Mary Ann from buying it totally.

Standing, Mary Ann excused herself to go to the restroom. Mainly she wanted to get away to lick the mental wounds Stephie had inflicted. Kyle's stepmother obviously didn't want her there.

In the hallway leading to the ladies' room, she noticed her bracelet had come undone and somehow slipped off her wrist. Glancing back, she spotted her favorite piece and hurried to retrieve it.

As Mary Ann bent over to pick it up, she caught Stephie's irritated voice and realized she was the topic of conversation. It was bad manners to eavesdrop, but that wasn't enough of a deterrent when Stephie already thought the worst of her.

***

"Really, Kyle, have you no sense of class?" Stephie raised a brow and looked down her nose at Kyle in her usual condescending fashion. The tactic had never worked on him, but that never stopped her from using it. "One would think you're dating her purely to annoy us."

Stephie was in rare form tonight. Kyle had put up with enough of her innuendoes to last him a lifetime. How in the hell did his dad put up with her? "Does it annoy you?" He crossed his legs at the ankles and leaned back, sporting a bored expression. Thank

115

God he only had to endure her presence occasionally.

"You know it does."

He flashed a sardonic smile and, knowing it was rude but unable to resist pulling her chain, he said, "Then I've achieved something."

"The next thing I know you'll be marrying her just to get back at your father for marrying me."

"I hadn't thought about that, but now that you mention it, it sounds like an awesome idea."

"I'd like to eat my dinner in peace without you two squabbling, if you don't mind," his father interjected.

Kyle cleared his throat. He shouldn't let Stephie get to him. "Sorry, Dad." He turned in time to see Mary Ann standing a few feet away, her eyes big as saucers, the pain etched into her face telling him quite clearly she'd heard the entire exchange.

"Shit," he said under his breath as he shoved away from the table.

When Stephie obviously realized Mary Ann had overheard her snide comments, she glanced at her husband. "I didn't know she was standing right there."

"Didn't you? I believe you knew exactly what you were doing. It's time you stopped trying to turn Kyle into someone he's not."

Kyle heard his father, but was too focused on catching up with Mary Ann to take it all in.

"Mary Ann, stop," he said, reaching out to grab her elbow to halt her retreat as she made it to the restaurant's entrance.

She wouldn't meet his eyes. "I want to go home."

"I'll drive you."

Shaking her head, she started for the exit. "I can take a taxi."

"You don't need to." Kyle helped her open the door when she seemed bound and determined to leave. Once outside where they had a bit more privacy, he said, "My stepmother overstepped her bounds." He let out an audible sigh. "As usual."

"Is she right?"

"What do you mean?"

She glanced up at him, her expression cold. "Are you dating me to annoy her?" The tilt of her head indicated the restaurant door. "Or maybe I'm one of your causes."

"No. God, no."

"Then what are we doing, Kyle?" Her gaze pleaded as much as her tone. "Where do we go from here?"

He swallowed hard, knowing exactly what she wanted. She wanted to hear him say he loved her. But he couldn't. Saying the words would set too much in motion. Now that push came to shove, he wasn't ready to go there yet. "I don't know," he said truthfully. Maybe there *was* a bit of truth to Stephie's statement. Had Kyle picked her to irritate his father?

The indecision must have shown in his eyes because she shook her head slowly. "I know where I want to go, and I want someone who doesn't hesitate to go there with me."

She turned and walked away. Kyle let her go as an ache began to build inside his gut. The ache of loss. Still, he did nothing to stop her.

If she wasn't willing to wait for him, she didn't really love him. The minute the thought was out, he knew he was lying to himself. "Wait," he yelled as she climbed into a taxi. She didn't wait. Didn't even look back at him. Just gave the driver instructions and stared straight ahead as if he didn't exist.

As Mary Ann drove out of his life, the pain in his heart grew. Everything he'd feared was happening. She was leaving him, just like his mother had. Just like his high school sweetheart had, only this time he was the one who pushed love away. It was better to feel pain now when he could tolerate it, than later after he'd fallen more deeply in love with her.

For a long time, he stood there staring at the empty street. Unwilling to go back inside and be civil to his stepmother, Kyle handed the valet his ticket. Let his dad handle her as he always did. He was done trying.

SANDY LOYD

Chapter 15

The week dragged. On Friday, Kyle pushed away from his desk after finishing the last round of paperwork. As he reached for his briefcase, his dad appeared at the door.

"I'm sorry, son." Ronald stepped into the room and closed the door. "I never meant for last weekend to happen."

"Why does she do it?" He didn't need to mention Stephie's name. They both knew who he was talking about.

Ronald shook his head and sighed. "Because I let her get away with it."

Kyle glanced at him without bothering to check his annoyance. "I can't believe you actually admitted it."

"Why? It's the truth." Ronald's shoulders sagged and he walked farther into the room. "But no more," he said, sitting in the chair in front of Kyle's desk. "I've taken steps to deal with her."

In no mood to be nice, Kyle reached for his jacket. "Look, Dad, I was on my way out. I appreciate the apology." He started for the door. "But it's not necessary." He stopped with his hand on the knob and turned back. "And it's about twenty years too late."

"I realize that. It's why I'm here now."

Narrowing his eyes into suspicious slits, he tried to figure out exactly what his dad was after. "Do you think an apology this late can change everything and make us a big, happy family?"

"No. But it's a start." When Kyle was about to tell him not to waste his breath, Ronald put up a hand. "Please hear me out. What can it hurt but a little time?"

Shrugging, Kyle glanced at his watch. "You have five minutes." He crossed his arms and glared at his dad. "Which is double what you usually allow me."

Ronald shot him an apologetic grimace. "Touché. I deserved that."

The defeated curve of his father's shoulders, along with the hint of sadness lurking in his dad's pleading gaze, stopped Kyle from verbally beating him down further. "I'm sorry. That was a low blow and if you're willing to talk, the least I can do is listen."

"Thank you." Ronald's lips flattened into a straight line. "It's time to come clean. If you hate me afterward, it won't change anything, will it?"

"I don't hate you, Dad, but I'm tired of trying to get your attention." Kyle offered a rueful smile. "I can finally live without it." A sense of peace filled him when he realized it was the truth. "Stephie's your problem, not mine."

"Sit down, son," Ronald said. "What I have to say doesn't concern Stephie. This is about your mother."

"Mom? What about her?"

Ronald pointed to Kyle's desk. "It isn't an easy topic for me to discuss, so I'd rather you be sitting."

Kyle slowly made his way to his chair and sat. "Okay, I'm listening," he said, glancing at his father expectantly, keeping all emotion off his face. "It's definitely time to talk about Mom."

"I loved your mother with my entire being. She was the light of my life, but she was also responsible for some of my darkest moments."

"What are you saying," Kyle asked. Surely he wasn't blaming his mother for their problems?

"She was sick, Kyle." Ronald's tortured gaze sought his. "Your mother suffered from bipolar disorder. That's a mental—"

"I'm familiar with the disorder," Kyle said, cutting him off. One of his kids was a manic depressive. "I also know it can be corrected with medication."

"The medications have improved tremendously in twenty-three years. Back then, she hated being on them and would continually stop taking them. Said she didn't feel normal." He quit talking and stared down at the floor.

The desire to get up and walk out was a strong one, but Kyle just sat there eyeing his father intently. "If she was sick, then why did you tell her to leave?" he blurted out before he lost his courage to say what he should have said right after his mother died.

That got his dad's attention. "What are you talking about?"

"Mom. On the night she died, you told her to get out. I want to know why." When Ronald's questioning gaze snapped to his eyes, he swallowed hard. "I saw you two fight. From my hiding place, I heard every word."

Stiffening, his father sat up straighter and stared into space as his expression tightened. Finally, he sighed. "Because I was afraid if she didn't leave then, she'd wait until I was gone and take you with her."

"Would that have been so bad?"

"Yes. Your mother was not well enough to take care of a child without help, mainly because of her inconsistency with taking her meds." He paused. "She'd been acting erratically, so I suspected she'd gone off them, but I didn't realize the duration. Apparently, it had been awhile, based on the autopsy. Earlier that day, she'd threatened to take you and leave. I told her over my dead body. Over the course of the afternoon, she became more agitated. I feared her ranting would wake you, so I told her to get out and not to come back until she could get herself under control with her medication. Usually the threat was enough to get her to back down."

Kyle absorbed this stoically, remembering that night. His dad's confession explained a lot. Though he'd seen and heard everything from his hiding spot, he'd been too young to understand about mental illness and medication, so he'd forgotten that part of the fight. "You let her go, knowing she was a danger to herself?"

"That's just it. I didn't know. I was young and ignorant of the disease, and had no idea how bad it had escalated until she was gone." He dropped his head into his hands and wiped at his face. His shoulders slumped in resignation as he lifted his gaze. "I was responsible for her wrapping herself around that telephone pole. But I couldn't let her take you too."

As the meaning of his confession sank in, Kyle asked, "Why didn't you tell me this earlier?" Like twenty years earlier.

"Guilt." Ronald's expression turned self-deprecating. "And cowardice. At first, I'd convinced myself it was because I didn't want to ruin your opinion of her. But then I realized I was afraid of losing you by letting you know I was the one who shoved her out the door."

"I already knew, Dad," Kyle admitted.

Silently, Ronald studied his face as sorrow filled his eyes. "I'm sorry, son. The true tragedy is that what I feared most became reality." His hand went to the bridge of his nose, where he spent a few seconds rubbing with his forefinger and thumb. "Can you ever forgive me?"

"I don't know." Kyle's entire world was suddenly tossed upside down. It was all too much. For two-thirds of his life he'd believed his dad uncaring, but seeing such pain in his father's expression jumbled his feelings into chaos. "Where does Stephie come in?" he asked when he could think again. Unable to hold the question inside because he was dying to know, he added, "Why did you marry her and forget about me?"

"I didn't forget about you, I couldn't deal with my guilt. It was easier to pass you off to your grandmother, something I'll regret until my dying day. You deserved a full-time dad."

His admission did much to ease the ache in his heart over being second place behind his stepmother. "I still don't understand why you married her."

"She's an asset to me and my company."

"What does that mean?"

"It means we understand each other." He sighed. "She doesn't ask too much of me and I don't ask too much of her."

"Sounds like a hollow life."

His father smiled. "No different from yours, I'd imagine."

"I don't follow you."

"Your grandmother believes I remained silent to keep a wall up between us, which is a dead-on assessment on two counts, I've since discovered."

When Kyle didn't respond, Ronald grunted. "I let Stephie criticize you because to speak up would point a finger in my direction. If she kept us apart, then I wouldn't have to admit to the other."

"That's so sad, Dad."

Ronald nodded. "It's easy to keep yourself from caring too much. I should know. After your mother died, I became a master at it. It's like sticking your toe in the water and testing the temperature without ever having to get wet. At any time, you can decide to walk away if it's too hot or too cold. The hard part is jumping into the deep end and having to swim."

"That's your life. Not mine."

"It's both our lives. It's my legacy to you, one that shouldn't be repeated."

When Kyle's gaze turned questioning, Ronald said, "I saw how you were with Mary Ann. It's obvious you love her. She's a keeper. Reminds me of your mother when things were good between us." Ronald's face softened into a smile. "Don't lock yourself off like I've done. I loved your mother dearly and don't regret a minute we shared together, even the horrible times when she'd go a little crazy." He glanced at his hands as his smile faded into a firm line.

"I've closed myself off from Stephie to keep from feeling pain, and look where it's gotten me. Nowhere."

He looked up at Kyle. Honesty shimmered in his eyes. "I'm not doing it any longer. We're seeing a marriage counselor. After all, we are committed to each other. And we have Bradley to think of. I only hope you'll forgive me. If you can't, then at the very least, I hope you can learn from my mistake."

Ronald rose to his feet.

As he started for the door, a chunk of ice surrounding Kyle's heart melted. He was tired of living with the anger. Life was too short as it was. Ronald had taken a giant leap to building a better relationship. The least he could do was meet him halfway. If anything, it would be the first step to forgiveness. "Wait, Dad."

Ronald stopped in midstride and turned back. Kyle rushed up to him and opened his arms to give him a hug, but his father was already engulfing his shoulders. For the first time since he could remember, Kyle felt a sense of peace toward his dad as he hugged him in return. "I love you, Dad. Thanks for trusting me with the truth."

"Don't make my mistake," he whispered. "Follow your heart and open it as wide as you can. Yet be prepared for a few hardships along the way." Ronald released his hold, and capturing his gaze, he smiled. "Those are what allow you to appreciate the good times."

"I'll think about it." Kyle watched him leave his office, then grabbed his briefcase and followed him out. The entire time he walked to his car, he wondered if he had the guts to jump into the deep end with Mary Ann. Of course, that was assuming Mary Ann would even speak to him. Suddenly, he understood his father's motivations more clearly.

In particular, he realized his motivations were no different, especially since it would be a hell of a lot easier to walk away than risk any more of his heart.

Chapter 16

Mary Ann headed south to Union City, driving well under the speed limit, in no big rush to spend a few hours with her boisterous family. The Murphys occasionally had get-togethers for Saturday brunch. Mary Ann was usually the first to arrive of her sisters and brothers, who always attended. Except for Tom, an Air Force pilot still stationed in Afghanistan. Today, she was intentionally late.

Six days had passed since her mad exodus from the disastrous dinner with Kyle, his father, and stepmother. Definitely not enough time to come to terms with the outcome, when it still hurt to remember their conversation. She hadn't heard one peep from Kyle. Nor did she expect to.

As she parked in her parents' driveway, she wondered if all rich people were so condescending.

Smiling brightly, she walked through the door and was greeted with either hugs or enthusiastic shouts from the family room where, by the sounds of the cheers, a football game played on the TV. The warmth in the greeting was the complete opposite of the cold reception of last Sunday night. Mary Ann's smile became more genuine. Money couldn't buy her kind of happiness.

"Where's Kyle today?" Her mother looked around outside before shutting the door, then glanced back at Mary Ann, an expectant expression sliding over her face.

"He's with his kids today," she lied, not wanting to discuss her breakup with Kyle or what led to it.

"What's this? A new boyfriend?" Caryn, her older sister by fifteen months, took her coat and proceeded to hang it up. Caryn was also the one who excelled at everything, including the college degree and the engagement ring, neither of which Mary Ann possessed.

She ignored her sister's pointed look without responding and veered toward the family room, using the noise and activity as a buffer. Mary Ann loved her sisters and brothers, but hated it when her failures became the topic of conversation. They all tended to rush to defend or advise. Each and every sibling would chime in with an opinion of what she should or shouldn't do.

"Your sister's dating a very nice man," she overheard her mother say to Caryn.

With an inward groan, she rolled her eyes. "That's the problem with being in the middle of nine kids."

"What?" Colleen said. "I didn't quite catch that."

Mary Ann glanced back and her expression became more innocent. "Nothing." When she spotted Sam on the sofa, sandwiched between her husband, James, and her mother, Vickie, she heaved a sigh of relief. "Hey, Sam. How's it going?" If anything could keep the Murphys off her back, it would be the added company. Holding on to her smile, she greeted James and Vickie as Sam looked up.

"Hey, Mar. I'm fine," Sam said. "Except I'd be a lot happier if SC were winning."

Her smile spread. Her best friend was a diehard University of Southern California fan. "Who are they playing?"

"Vanderbilt."

"Ah," she said. That explained why James looked so happy. Football was something both took seriously. Sam always grumbled about James selling out because he rooted for a Tennessee team rather than California's own.

"Mimosas are in the kitchen," her dad said, holding up his drink. "Vickie brought the champagne."

"Thanks." Mary Ann headed for the kitchen and poured herself some orange juice, but refrained from adding the champagne. She wasn't in the mood to celebrate.

Sam had followed. "So, what's up?" She looked pointedly at the glass in her hand. "More importantly, why are you avoiding the good stuff?"

"Don't make a big deal out of it," she said, signaling toward the other room with the tilt of her head. "I don't want them knowing I'm upset. Otherwise, I'll get the third degree." God only knew what her family would say when they discovered she'd made another mistake by falling in love with the wrong man.

"Did something happen between you and Kyle?" Sam poured herself half a glass of orange juice, then filled the rest of the space with champagne. "Where is he today? I thought for sure he'd come. Maggie says he's big on family."

"Apparently Maggie doesn't know him very well."

"Now I have my answer," Sam said before taking a drink.

"It's a long story. Plus, I'd rather it not be a part of Murphy mania." The term she and Sam used to describe the latest family gossip.

Colleen walked into the kitchen. "I was wondering where you disappeared to." She glanced at the glass in her hand and smiled. "So, what happened with Kyle that caused you to need fortification?"

"I'm only having orange juice."

"Now I'm positive something happened." Two of her sisters entered her line of vision as her mother added, "You might as well tell me because I won't stop badgering until you do."

"What's this?" Bridget asked. Her youngest sister halted in the doorway, a nosy grin splitting her face in two. "Whatever it is, it sounds juicy."

Mary Ann blew at her bangs. "Why do you have to assume the worst?"

Colleen sent her a questioning look. "I didn't mean to upset you," she said after studying her face as if some hidden secret were buried there. She eventually turned to her two other daughters and her expression hardened. "Leave Mary Ann alone. When she's ready to talk, she will." Colleen then proceeded to herd them out of the room.

The second they were all out of earshot, Sam grabbed her shoulders and gave her a shake. "What in the hell is going on between you and Kyle?" she whispered.

"We broke up," Mary Ann said. The admission was like unplugging a cooler of ice water, allowing the story to gush out in a flood of words. When finished, she glanced at Sam to view her reaction.

Sam wrapped an arm around her shoulders. "That doesn't sound like Kyle." Squeezing reassuringly, she added, "Maggie filled me in a little on his background. He doesn't have a warm, loving family to show him the way. Grant him a little latitude and be patient. Kyle's worth the effort."

"I feel like such a loser, though," Mary Ann admitted.

"Why? Because you care for someone? I can understand beating yourself up over Steve. He was an ass who didn't deserve you. Don't rush to judgment against Kyle because of Steve's sins."

"I'm not."

"Yes, you are. What's more, you're running away."

She held her head high. "No, I'm not."

Sam eyed her without blinking. "Be honest, Mar. If not with me, then with yourself."

The command brought her up short. Was she running? She pushed a strand of hair behind her ear and glanced at her hand. "I'm afraid of getting hurt again," she finally confessed.

"Now, the truth comes out." Sam snorted. "When's your next dance class?"

"Tonight. Why?"

"Because you are going to be there."

"I can't go. Not without Kyle, and I'm sure he won't be there."

"Take a chance. What can it hurt but a little embarrassment?" Sam rubbed her hands as a smug expression landed on her face. "If it doesn't work out, you'll never see those people again."

"Okay," Mary Ann agreed.

"Think fast." A sponge football hit her in the head as Kevin's voice registered. "You two interested in a quick game of touch football?"

Mary Ann grabbed it after it bounced on the counter behind her. She aimed for her brother, who sidestepped right as Colleen entered the room. "Great idea," she said, suddenly feeling as if a weight had been lifted off her shoulders.

One-handed, Colleen caught the ball and glared at Kevin. "Not in the house."

There was a park across the street. One by one, the Murphys exited the house along with Sam and James as Colleen said, "You have exactly thirty minutes before the food is ready."

"Do you need any help?" Mary Ann said, turning back.

Smiling, her mother shook her head. "You can help me serve. I'll call you when I need you."

Mary Ann made her way to Colleen and gave her a big hug along with a kiss.

Her mom blinked and said in a flustered tone, "What was that for?"

"Because I love you. I'm lucky to have you as a mother and be part of this family."

Chapter 17

Waiting was definitely the pits.

Mary Ann paced. She stopped and stared at the door. As she rolled her shoulders to relieve some of the nervous tension, she wondered if Kyle would even bother to show up, or why Sam had insisted she be here tonight. To prove her wrong, she'd come.

Now she realized she'd made a huge mistake. She was chicken and she had been running away. Worse, the urge to run now was greater than ever. Kyle hadn't rejected her. She'd pushed him away before he had a chance to either catch up with her or reject her. Mary Ann felt rather foolish for letting her insecurities get the best of her again.

The door to the dance studio opened and there he stood. Damn, he looked good as he stepped inside. His gaze sought hers, one that spoke a thousand words and all of them expressing love.

"Class." Frau Haubner clapped, drawing their focus. After going through her usual spiel, the instructor glanced at Kyle. Then her gaze scoured the room, eventually landing on her. "I have a special treat tonight. In my last session, I was privileged to meet two very gifted dancers. I haven't asked them outright, but I was hoping they would dance their waltz so the entire class can see what can happen when passion and technique come together to form art."

Frau Haubner held out her hand. "Mary Ann and Kyle, please step forward and show them how it's done."

Shy all of a sudden, Mary Ann could only move slowly, putting one foot in front of the other. Heavens, she wasn't sure she would survive being in Kyle's arms and having him reject her love. No! She would not think about defeat. Not now when she'd come so far. If he walked away, then it was his loss.

Her entire carriage straightened as the thought traveled down her spine to her toes. She was worth love and she knew how to give it. If he couldn't accept what she had to offer, then so be it.

It had taken almost two years to crawl to this point. Finally here, she fully understood that Steve had done her a favor. She'd never be happy with a man who had no integrity. Kyle was that man, and she would dance the waltz of her life, conveying her feelings with each step.

All too soon, he stood in front of her. "Hey, gorgeous."

"Hey, gorgeous yourself."

"Are you ready to show them how to dance?"

"I thought you'd never ask."

He swept her into his arms and glided her around the room. The music flowed through her, and with every touch, every glance his way, she extended her body to show him what he meant to her.

In turn, Kyle answered, his gaze throwing her thoughts into chaos, but still the melody played on as Kyle guided her through their routine, one she'd never forget.

He spun her in the last turn and her heart lurched, because no one could miss the love shining in his eyes. The dance ended as Kyle bent to kiss her. "I love you," he whispered. "I'll always love you."

"Bravo." Frau Haubner's German-accented cheer was followed by a huge round of applause. "You never cease to amaze me," she added. "Your waltz was a love story in motion."

Kyle tugged on Mary Ann's arm to lift her out of the ending dip. They bowed together. As with the week before, everything inside her wanted him.

"Come on, let's get out of here." Still holding her hand, Kyle tugged gently to get her moving with him. Near the door, he turned back to a stunned Frau Haubner. "Thank you, Frau Haubner, for teaching me the basics. I think I can handle things from here."

"But…but…but…" It took her a few more buts before she added, "What about your free lessons?"

"Give them to the Hendersons. They need to learn a few things about passion."

Chapter 18

At bingo a week later, Kyle and Mary Ann showed up at the already full table.

"Sorry we're late."

"Don't worry about it," Irma said.

As two extra chairs appeared, Irma and Maggie scooted closer together along with the other occupants at the table, making room for them.

Kyle held out Mary Ann's chair and sat down next to her. He glanced around the table amid greetings and smiles. "We have some news." He cleared his throat, then looked at Mary Ann. "Do you want to do the honors?"

Mary Ann smiled slyly and set her hand on the table.

"Oh my God." Colleen caught her daughter's gaze, her eyes filling with tears as the oohs and aahs surrounded them. "Congratulations."

Kyle focused on Grams to see her reaction.

Grams nodded her approval as Maggie winked. "Do I know how to pick 'em or what?"

"You certainly do," Grams said.

Colleen finished wiping her eyes, then glanced up. "I have seven more at home who need to find partners. I can get them to come to bingo, if you think you can help."

"That sounds like a challenge," Maggie said, grinning.

"You'd think a grandchild would be enough to keep her busy," Kyle said under his breath to Mary Ann. Judith, Maggie's daughter-in-law, had given birth to a healthy baby boy six months earlier.

"I caught that. I can do both." She rubbed her hands together and said in a gloating tone, "I love it when a plan comes together."

Mary Ann rolled her eyes. "I'm going to have to warn my siblings. You people are ruthless."

"Now, Mary Ann," her mother said, waving the comment away. "Don't go ruining our fun. Besides, I don't hear you two complaining."

Kyle's quick laugh burst free. "You're right," he said at the same time Mary Ann said, "Have at it." She added, "You've already used dance lessons, so you'll have to come up with something else."

"All the more challenging," Maggie said with a laugh.

As the others joined in, Kyle leaned toward Mary Ann and whispered, "I can't wait to see what happens next."

~~THE END~~

Thank you for reading *Dancing with an Angel*. I hope you enjoyed it!

• Would you like to know when my next book is available? Simply e-mail me at sandyloyd@twc.com and I'll add you to my list. Follow me on twitter at @sloydwrites, or like my Facebook page at http://facebook.com/sloydwrites.

• Reviews help other readers find books. I appreciate all reviews, whether positive or negative.

• Share it with a friend!

•You've just read Book Four of The California Series. The first three stories are now bundled and available on Amazon - http://amzn.to/1bhetOm.

If you'd like to read more of my work, turn the page for the first chapter of The Sin Factor, my first Romantic Suspense, a book that doesn't skimp on romance and one where the hero and heroine fall in love while solving a mystery.

About the Author

Sandy Loyd is a Western girl through and through. Born and raised in Salt Lake City, she's worked and lived in some fabulous places in the US, including South Florida. She now resides in Kentucky and writes full time. As much as she loves her current hometown, she misses the mountains and has to go back to her roots to get her mountain and skiing fix at least once a year, otherwise her muse suffers.

As a sales rep for a major manufacturer, she's traveled extensively throughout the US, so she has a million stored memories to draw from for her stories. She spent her single years in San Francisco and considers that city one of America's treasures, comparable to no other city in the world. Her California Series, starting out with Winter Interlude, are all set in the Bay Area.

Sandy is now an empty nester who has published twelve full length novels—five contemporary romances, four romantic mystery/suspense/thrillers, and a series that starts out with a time travel and follows up with two historical romances in the past. She strives to come up with fun characters—people you would love to call friends. And we all know friends have their baggage and when we discover what makes them tick, we come to love them even more. She doesn't skimp on the romance. And because she loves puzzles, she doesn't skimp on intrigue, either. Yet whether romantic suspense, contemporary romance, or historical romance, she always tries to weave a warm love story into her work, while providing enough twists and turns to entertain any reader.

The Sin Factor

When Jeffrey Sinclair is forced to unravel the puzzle of who is stealing from his company and why, he gets caught up in a deadly game, one perpetrated by those who've vowed to protect our freedom. He and his colleagues infiltrate the life of the one person they feel is the link to solving the mystery, Avery Montgomery. Avery is the widow of the last known person to have their devices in his possession before he died.

Avery is a woman heroes marry and protect for life, and Sin's never been the protecting, hero type, not like her dead husband was. When it becomes obvious that someone is threatening Avery, *Sin* believes it's for the same reasons he and his partners are interested in her. He follows the twists and turns of the chase and does everything in his power to keep her safe while fighting to keep the attraction he feels in check. And in the end he realizes that somehow he's become exactly what he never thought possible...*her hero.*

Chapter 1

Tree branches swayed, bending to the will of a brisk breeze. Dusk prevailed—that moment in time when it was neither dark nor light.

Avery Montgomery slowly turned to peer at the surrounding landscape, scrutinizing the trees and brush to her left and directly behind her where the gravesites ended. In front of her and still visible in the twilight row after row of pearly headstones fanned out in precise lines.

Shivering, she rubbed her arms.

She waited.

As if her thoughts had ordered the air to still, the leaves stopped their movement. For endless minutes all was calm, until a prickly sensation at the back of her neck indicated his presence, a feeling she'd had before.

Every nerve ending in her body stood at alert. Still waiting. For what, she had no idea.

She closed her eyes and chastised herself. After all, she stood in a cemetery—Arlington, at that. She took a deep breath. The smell of fresh-cut grass eased the eeriness of standing so close to the remains of dead soldiers.

Yet, the feeling of being watched didn't dissipate. Did he realize she sensed him watching? Why assume it was a he? She pretended not to notice. If she pretended hard enough, then *he* wasn't real. Pretending had become a huge part of her life in recent years. She had no reason to doubt her pretense wouldn't work. It had all those other nights she'd stood staring at the graves of two men who'd died almost two months ago.

Avery's focus returned to the headstones. She concentrated on the chiseled words.

Major Michael Andrew Montgomery.

Major Marshall Compton Crandall.

One had been her husband for most of her adult life and the other had been his best friend. Both died serving their country, a sacrifice honored with an Arlington burial.

She glanced toward the heavens. If only she could go back in time and undo her past. Unfortunately, it was written, never to be undone, and she would have to live with the consequences.

"You look so sad."

She pivoted and leaned toward the voice. The soft sound penetrated her ears and reached into her soul, as if directed solely, intimately to her. Squinting, she could only see shadows of trees in the now moonlit darkness.

Ignore it. It isn't real.

Avery shrugged it off and sighed. She was obviously hallucinating. She stood alone in the middle of a cemetery, and cemeteries were notorious for evoking weird feelings.

"I guess I am sad," she whispered, going against her mind's reasoning because she felt compelled to answer. Oh dear God. She was going crazy. Why did she have this overwhelming need to hear his voice again? Avery's narrowed gaze searched the darkened brush once more. She spent a moment listening. When no other noise sounded, she turned back to the two graves.

In seconds, tears emerged, and it dawned on her that she *was* sad…grief-stricken…for what would never be…for what her transgressions had manifested.

"I'm so sorry, Mike. I never meant to make such a mess of things." More tears trickled. Her husband had gone to his grave with no other word than the confusing letter he'd sent right before he died. She'd never know if he'd forgiven her or not.

Stop it. It's too late for forgiveness.

She wiped away her tears.

A ping sounded a few feet away. In the next instant, a force hit her from behind, throwing her off balance. Her legs buckled from the weight. Too stunned to do anything but put out her hands to soften the fall, she hit the ground with a hard thud.

"*Oomph*," she cried out none too gracefully as the air escaped her chest. She slowly gained her wits and tried to move, but couldn't. Something…or someone…hampered her. A man. He rolled with her, using the headstones as a shield. A chunk of earth bounced off the ground only inches away and she identified the ping.

"My God! Those are bullets." Arms flailing, she struggled to get up.

"Stay down," he said, his voice low but urgent.

She couldn't do much else with the man sprawled on top of her. She recognized her figment's voice. A living, breathing human voice.

"This is Arlington," she whispered, fighting to rein in her out-of-control imagining of a gun-toting terrorist hiding in the bushes taking potshots. "Why is someone shooting?"

~~~~~

Jeffrey Sinclair caught the panic in her voice. "I don't know why, but I intend to find out." He shifted and covered her more protectively. Through layers of clothes, he felt her heartbeat race. Or was it his?

He managed to yank his radio out of his pocket and hit the button just as another bullet ricocheted off a headstone to his left. "Three shots fired." With his lips next to her ear, he kept his voice low. "As far as I can tell, from northwest of my position."

"On it," came the reply.

Silence prevailed. In those quiet seconds, the alert edge left his body in an exhale, but she remained as immobile as stone.

"You're safe," he assured her in a soothing tone. "I won't let anything happen to you." Sin wasn't the protecting type, but as the promise escaped his lips, he realized he meant every word.

She nodded and seemed to relax a bit. Her lemony scent blended with the dampened earth and invaded his nostrils. An inconvenient blast of awareness shot through him. As the danger diminished with each passing minute, leftover adrenaline had his heartbeat quickening, pumping more alertness through every vein and artery. He felt trapped in some kind of suspended time warp, intensifying the craziness of lying prone over some stranger. Well, not exactly a stranger. He knew enough, and though he couldn't deny an attraction to her, he damn sure hadn't expected Avery Montgomery to affect him like this.

Hold it together, Sin.

Remember why you're on top of her in the first place. Someone shot at her. Unfortunately, his mental commands couldn't extinguish her warmth radiating beneath him. The hard contours of his body dug into her softness, adding to his awareness…and his discomfort. He closed his eyes, willing Des to hurry, and forced himself to relax. To keep breathing.

Five…ten…twenty seconds ticked by and still nothing happened.

Finally, he lifted off her enough to let her roll onto her back but he wouldn't relinquish his protective posture. Damn. Not his smartest move because now she lay underneath him face up. Darkness obscured her full features, but he didn't need to see her to know she was gorgeous.

The rapid thumping of his heart continued to override the silence. With her head inches from his, the soft air of her even breathing caressed his neck. His blood pounded faster.

Don't think about it. Think about the situation. Where in the hell is Des?

Finally, the radio came alive again. "All clear. Whoever was shooting is long gone. I'll scout around a little more, see what I can find."

"Thanks, but be careful. It ruins my night when someone uses me for target practice," he answered.

Sin pushed up onto his forearms and looked down to see Avery suck in air and open her eyes. At the same time, the full moon came out of hiding and a bit of light reflected off her face, highlighting a frightened brown gaze. He began to pull away, but the glimpse of sadness he also saw stopped him cold. For long seconds their stares locked. Peering into such vivid, expressive eyes was the wrong thing to do, but he couldn't look away.

Her turbulent gaze spoke volumes, created a bond of sorts. A *mental connection*, for lack of a better term, that was damned unwelcome and tossed his thoughts into chaos. Questions that had rested on the tip of his tongue scattered to the far reaches of his mind.

Whoever said the eyes were the windows to the soul had it right. He didn't know her—they'd never met—but it was as if he'd known her forever. How stupid was that? Or maybe surreal. This entire scene had a dream-like quality to it.

Of its own accord, his gaze dropped inches lower, to her mouth. An incredibly beautiful mouth. He certainly wasn't considering doing something so stupid like kissing that mouth, was he? Yeah, because even as his brain shouted no, his body had other ideas. At that point, stupid just didn't seem to matter.

In slow motion, he lowered his head, giving her plenty of time to turn away.

Avery didn't move, yet that expressive gaze seemed to beg him for something, which spurred him to continue. She still didn't pull away even when his mouth hovered over hers before grazing back and forth. The not quite kisses sent searing flashes of heat straight through him. When her lips connected with his, he wrapped his arms around her in an effort to bring her closer. Never had a kiss seemed so elemental...like breathing. Like being in heaven.

"I don't see any shell casings. I'm betting the bullets came from a high-powered rifle," his radio squawked. "So, I'll try to find the bullets."

Instantly, he broke the kiss and felt a twinge of regret.

Whether it was for the interruption or his impulsive act, he wasn't certain.

As the voice seeped into Avery's thoughts, reality hit. Her entire body stiffened. Panic re-entered her consciousness, along with total embarrassment, as the reason she lay underneath a stranger in a cemetery in the first place returned. Someone had shot at her. She had to get out of here. Get home and make sure her son was okay.

"Sin?" the same voice asked. "You there?"

He lifted off her and said into his radio, "I'm here," then rolled away to say more.

Sin? Was that his name? How fitting. He truly was some specter sent from hell to torment her. She wasn't someone who rolled around in graveyards with strange men after being shot at. She was a grieving widow. A mother, for heaven's sake. Didn't she have enough to feel guilty over?

"Are you okay?"

She glanced up at the sound and caught him eyeing her with concern etched into his expression. *Are you okay? Question of the year.* No, she was not okay. She'd never be okay. To prove it, she'd just spent the last few minutes in mindless absurdity, wishing the kiss with a complete stranger could go on forever. She nodded and worked at pretending she wasn't staring into the most incredible gaze, one that saw more than she cared to expose.

Avery rubbed her temples. Who the hell was he? Whoever he was, he'd probably saved her life. Risking another glance, she took a deep breath. Even in the shadows, she noted an arresting presence. His face wasn't pretty. Too many angles and hard edges…adding to his undeniable maleness. And he had a power about him that held her in its force, which only increased her internal turbulence. No wonder she'd felt protected underneath him and totally safe, which made no sense at all.

In the blink of an eye, her fear returned full force. She was totally aware of her vulnerability. His size, dwarfing her five feet nine inches, suddenly made her feel defenseless.

"You sure?" He waited a moment, watching her closely. When she didn't offer a reply, he stood, bent to help her, and flashed a quick, lopsided grin. "Sorry about that kiss. I got carried away."

Avery took his offered hand and allowed him to pull her up. "I…um…no problem." What else could she say? She'd gotten carried away too? He probably thought kissing men she'd never met in cemeteries after being shot at was her norm.

Someone shot at her.

"I need to go." She yanked her hand out of his grasp. *Home.* Everything would be okay if she could just make it home and check on Andy. That thought became a driving force.

"Hold on." He reached for his wallet, retrieved a business card, and held it out. "My name's Jeffrey Sinclair."

Avery stopped her retreat long enough to take the card.

So his name was Sinclair, not Sin. The fact didn't ease her conscience any after what she'd just done. Sin or no Sin, she'd made a complete fool of herself. She had to get out of here.

Despite a million questions peppering her brain just then, she turned and darted out of instinct, disturbed by the kiss as much as what preceded it.

Never in a billion years would she consider herself someone who'd meet an unknown man's mouth so crazily. Not when, according to Mike, she was frigid and never got emotional. But here she was an emotional mess and the thought only swamped her with more emotion.

She veered in the direction of her parked car as more humiliation rose up over her reaction to a complete stranger. His presence had made her feel cherished. That alone seemed totally illogical, but when he'd bent to kiss her, she hadn't been able to turn away. In those few seconds she'd felt more alive than she had in fifteen years. Mike's kisses had never generated such a response.

"Wait. I'd like to talk to you. Make sure you're safe."

That same gripping, almost disturbing voice carried on the wind. She fought to ignore the urgent tone, but somehow the quality reached past the physical, just as his concerned stare had done, touching something deep inside of her she didn't want touched.

"No..." she said over her shoulder. "I'm fine. Really. I appreciate your help, but I've got to get home." By the time she made it to her car she was running. She slowed her steps and looked back. He'd made no attempt to follow, thank God, just stood and watched her in the moonlit shadows. With her focus still on him, she hit the keyless entry. Lights flashed and the locks snapped up. She scrambled inside.

In seconds, Avery had her seat belt fastened and the car started. She worked to keep her foot steady as she put the car in gear and sped off.

Maybe running away denoted cowardice, but cowardice was the least of her troubles.

~~~

"What happened? Why is she leaving?"

Jeffrey Sinclair ignored the questions, still keeping a protective watch as her car's taillights flashed brighter when she slowed to turn left onto the main road leading out of the cemetery.

"Sin?" Desmond Phillips strode up to him. "Why didn't you stop her?"

He turned to his business partner and grunted. "She's not going anywhere."

"But it's obvious at this point she's part of it. She's been here every night we've staked out the gravesite. This would've been the perfect opportunity to discover what she knows."

"It can wait. What I want to know is…why would someone try and kill her?"

"Diversionary tactic," Des spit out. "Had to be. A high-powered rifle with a silencer? He was probably using a scope. Had a clean shot and missed. On purpose. To draw us out. Which in my book indicates some kind of involvement."

"Maybe." Sin's gaze moved to the now empty street. He clenched a fist, hating that he had no answers. Why had he spoken to her? Even more disturbing, why had he kissed her…her, of all women?

He snorted. Hell, he knew why. He hadn't been able to stop, that's why. Now, more than ever, she intrigued him. Each and every evening she'd made her nightly visits, he'd stationed himself just feet away. Watching…waiting…wanting.

"Shit," he whispered, then shook his head. Why deny his attraction? She was one gorgeous woman with curves in all the right places. He'd dealt with attraction before and never lost his head. Not like tonight, when she'd seemed so forlorn, peering at him with those haunting eyes, begging him to give in to the need.

Sin's fingernails dug deeper into his palms to the point of pain. He needed to find out if a connection existed between his company's stolen technology and the two dead Army officers. He couldn't let attractive females sidetrack him. As Des said, the lady now appeared to be involved. But to what extent?

"It's a waste of time to keep watching tonight. Nothing's going to happen now."

Des' voice yanked him back to the the reason they were lurking in a cemetery—the anonymous tip concerning the thefts from Sinclair Phillips & Coleman Electronics. "I agree." He nodded. "Whoever we were waiting for most likely got scared off with all the commotion."

"Had to be a setup." Des flashed a light onto the grass surrounding the headstones. The light caught something shiny. He stopped, then crouched and dug at the ground with his pocketknife.

"But why?" Sin drew a hand through his hair before resting it on the back of his neck. He began rubbing, trying to massage the kinks out. "What the hell have we stumbled into? Nothing makes sense. It's as if someone's playing a sick game. With our company. With our livelihood." The last phase of testing SPC's prototypes had been right on schedule until they'd gone missing. Now they had to deal with two more thefts.

"According to Colonel Williams' report, neither Major Crandall nor Major Montgomery fit the traitor profiles, and there's nothing to show their involvement." He watched Des extract a bullet from a nearby tree. Yet Montgomery had been in charge of testing the powerful light-driven tracking, listening, and recording devices. The dead major was the last known person to have them in his possession. In an attempt to learn all he could about him...and about *her*, Sin had memorized the pertinent details.

The stunning brunette's life read like a storybook romance on paper until Montgomery's death. Her deceased husband had been an all-American—athletic, good-looking, gifted—the poster boy for his college fraternity. The high school sweethearts had lived in the D.C. area, attending local Alexandria schools until college. He'd been two years ahead of her, graduating *summa cum laude* from Georgetown University before entering the Army.

"The colonel's right. Major Montgomery served ten years with a spotless record and several medals." Sin exhaled a resigned sigh. "He's a fricking war hero, not your usual scumbag who's sold his country's latest technology to the highest bidder."

Crandall's file read similarly. Despite the glowing words, Sin wasn't about to remove either officer from his short list of suspects. Military Intelligence had cleared them of all wrongdoing, but he and his partners couldn't afford to overlook any possibility. Too much was at stake.

"Maybe Montgomery needed the money."

"Money wasn't an issue." Sin met Des' gaze. "He came from old money, had access to a hefty trust fund. In fact, according to the file, several generations of Montgomerys earned money through interest, not hard work, and they all had one thing in common. They believed in giving back to society through public service, which plays into the war hero scenario."

He didn't want to think he harbored a prejudice toward dead heroes, but if Sin were totally honest, he'd have to admit to one. He'd always held such men in contempt, those born with not only the silver spoon but also the whole meal.

"Crandall didn't have Montgomery's megabucks, but their

backgrounds are parallel." Sin scrubbed a hand over his face. How could they be anything but heroes with that upbringing? Poster boys like Montgomery always had it easy, had their way paved, so much so they never had to truly fight for anything, always got their pick of everything just because of who they were…the best jobs with the best salaries attracting the best mates. The gutter Sin had climbed out of was totally at the other end of the spectrum. Unlike Montgomery or Crandall, he'd had to fight for everything.

Still, he dealt in logic and probabilities. Logically, the probabilities pointed to their innocence. As the colonel had stated during their last meeting, they had nil to go on as far as motive for tying either man to any treasonous treachery.

"The wife's involved. I know it. She's been here every night we have." Des pocketed the bullets and was now shining the light in the distance. "That means something."

"Coincidence. She *is* Montgomery's widow, after all."

"Too much coincidence for my liking. Who visits a gravesite so often these days?" Des' voice held disbelief. "And for so long?"

"A grieving widow whose husband recently died?"

"Maybe." Des nodded, still searching. "Or maybe she's in on it and the husband wasn't?"

Sin's gaze followed the beam of light hitting row after row of white stones. "She's definitely someone to question, but you can't really think she's involved in passing stolen technology?"

"I'm suspicious of everyone until I understand their motives," Des said. "If she were the target tonight, she'd be dead. And since she was alive enough to run away, my gut tells me she's part of the ploy to draw us out."

"You're too cynical. I'd think you'd be less biased, given your previous occupation," Sin teased. Such scorn resulted from Des' colossal mistake—marrying the wrong woman. Sin understood because he hadn't made the best of choices in a wife and had his own form of cynicism in dealing with the opposite sex. Still, he tried to be objective about it.

"Cynical or not, she's someone I want to interrogate." Des flicked off the light, but not before Sin caught the annoyance on his face.

Yep, Des' expression and tone indicated he'd already tried and convicted the lady. Sin wasn't inclined to condemn her so hastily. She just didn't seem like the traitor type. Having never finished her degree, she'd dropped out to marry Montgomery ten years ago and had a baby some seven months after the wedding.

Okay, so they had to get married, Sin thought. But that was kids being too hot and heavy and not using birth control. As far as he was concerned, being stupid and horny rarely led to selling out your country for monetary gain. He could even see how it might have happened, given Avery was a woman a man could lose his sanity over enough to forget the condom.

Lucky bastard…then again, maybe not so lucky as the guy's ashes are buried only two feet away and she's still vibrantly alive. If she were his, he wouldn't want to be separated from her for an instant.

"There has to be something," he whispered, not liking the ditch his thoughts had plowed into. "Some link with her dead husband to all of this."

"The wife *is* the connection, I'm telling you." Des pointed his flashlight at him as if making a point. "Wives, especially wives who've been married for so long, generally know not only where the bodies are buried, but how many and how deep."

Sin didn't reply. Right now the widow was the only solid lead they had.

"What about Williams? Maybe the military's made progress."

Sin frowned. "I doubt it." Colonel Williams was the Army official in charge of procuring and, in his mind, the person who supposedly got things done. Yet their Army liaison seemed useless in this situation. "He's not concerned with the theft, thanks to the fail-safe." If the prototypes landed in the wrong hands, they'd shut down without the proper sequence of numbers, and then self-destruct in fifteen hundred hours. Roughly seven days from now unless reactivated. "I rushed through the process and finalized our contract with the Army without thoroughly weighing the consequences. I certainly didn't think anyone would steal our product before it'd been fully tested." Sin sighed. "I thought the military would provide an element of security."

"It's understandable." Des clapped him on the back and grinned. "If you can't trust your government, who can you trust?"

"That's no excuse." Sin clenched his jaw. "Not for us. Not for me. Fulfilling this contract is too essential to our success." If the components weren't found in time, Williams would declare the project a failure. SPC Electronics, would be out millions, a loss they couldn't afford right now. Due to a provision in the contract stating SPC would be paid only upon confirmation of the technology working, there wasn't a damned thing Sin could do to stop the verdict.

"It's obvious the colonel has little interest in helping us." Sin shook his head in frustration. "He doesn't give a shit about whether or not we go under. His main concerns are saving face and not having to deal with military bureaucracy." With only a week left, the clock was ticking.

"I've still got a few friends on the force who owe me some favors." Des started walking toward the road. "I'll see if they can analyze these bullets." He patted his pocket. "Maybe we'll learn something useful."

Sin nodded and silently fell into step. At least Williams had provided him with a special sticker, the same one surviving spouses and family members received to enter the national cemetery after hours. "Maybe we should reconsider hiring a PI."

"We don't need outsiders." Des exhaled heavily. "They hold too many risks."

Sin nodded. Trust was the biggest issue, that and finding an investigator with the clearances necessary to deal with such sensitive information

"You're right, of course," Sin finally said, as they reached his car. When Des sent him a questioning look, he added, "We should talk to Mrs. Montgomery, and the sooner the better. Let's go back to the office to see if Eric's still there." Eric Coleman was their third partner.

He hit the keyless entry. Both opened their doors and slid inside simultaneously.

Sin wasn't looking forward to questioning the lady, given his earlier reaction. Maybe Des could do it without him. The minute the thought was out, he discarded it.

An ex-homicide detective, Des could spot inconsistencies and lies within seconds of talking to a person, a handy skill to possess due to the sensitive nature of their business. He was also a real pro at solving puzzles, but his friend wasn't what Sin would call a people person. With his square, muscular physique, he'd make a perfect bouncer in one of D.C.'s hottest nightclubs. And despite his stern, military-like bearing and short, dirty-blond buzz cut, both throwbacks from an early Marine Corps experience, the ladies must like him as he never lacked female company.

Sin watched Des snap his seat belt into place. Smiling, he started the engine and pulled onto the road. As he drove, his grin spread. He stifled a chuckle. Since Sin had already irritated the female in question with his actions, he couldn't risk poking the stick of Des' contemptuous personality at her and inflaming her further. SPC's chief of security might attract women like pollen-loaded daisies attracted bees, but his demeanor toward them was spiked with vinegar, not honey.

Questioning Mrs. Montgomery required teamwork, and they made a great team...sort of like good cop/bad cop when they interviewed prospective employees and clients.

Sin's breath came out in a long sigh. Unfortunately, he'd have to play his good cop part if he wanted to gain any useful information.

The memory of having her soft body under his flashed and he shifted uncomfortably on the leather seat.

"Damn," he said under his breath, punching the accelerator. No matter how hard he tried, the image wouldn't shake free. He didn't need any more complications.

And Avery Montgomery might prove to be a huge one.

~~~

Once Avery was miles down the road, well away from *him*, the incident replayed in her mind. *Incident?* She snorted, unable to describe what happened so simply.

An out-of-control kiss, maybe, but definitely not a mere incident. Guilt immersed her, filling her with more self-loathing. How could she have acted like a complete idiot...a lovesick fool without any restraint? She was a grieving widow, not some sex-starved hussy.

If that were true, then why did some part of her wonder what would have happened if they hadn't been interrupted? No. She hadn't liked kissing him. Fear, grief, and remorse had hit her all at once, creating her erratic behavior. Even so, she had to admit that Mike's kisses had never affected her like that.

At a red light, she closed her eyes for a brief second. Without the man's influence, she could finally think clearer. Someone had shot at her. Her earlier fear returned full force. Ice water ran through her veins replacing some of the other emotions. She stared in the rearview mirror searching for unseen threats and making note of those behind her.

When the light changed, her foot pushed the gas pedal. Hard. The car shot forward and sped up quickly. Her eyes kept checking the rearview mirror as she drove. One car in particular caught and held her attention. Her heartbeat increased.

Avery breathed out a relieved sigh the moment the car turned off, blocks from her house.

She pressed the garage door opener so that it was fully open when she pulled into her driveway at the rear of her Georgetown house. She didn't wait to hit the button to lower the door. As it closed, she put the car in park, turned off the engine, and stared at the wall in front of her.

Maybe she should have gone to the police. No. Arlington was military jurisdiction and she'd rather avoid anything to do with the military, especially Colonel Williams. She didn't fully trust him. Yet, what about the guy she'd kissed? Who was he?

Her hand went to her pocket, where she'd stashed his business card. She pulled it out and read: *Jeffrey Sinclair—CEO of SPC Electronics.* He said he wanted to talk to her. What was he doing at the gravesite, and not just tonight? She had no doubt he'd been there on those other nights she'd visited. And her biggest concern…who was shooting and why? Was she the target or was *he?*

Had to be him. And I got caught in some kind of crossfire.

Movement at the door separating the kitchen and the garage drew Avery's attention and Terry poked her head out after opening it.

Her sister watched for several minutes before she stepped forward and smiled. "Everything okay?" she asked, opening the car door when Avery made no attempt to move.

Avery couldn't help but notice how close the question was to what *he* had asked. As far as she was concerned, the answer hadn't changed. She wondered if she'd ever be *okay* again. She sighed, tucked the card away, intending to research the company later, and climbed out of the car.

"Sure." She returned the smile. Except it felt forced. Without meeting Terry's curious gaze, she grabbed her purse and headed inside. She needed to think…analyze her behavior…before she told anyone about the events of the past hour, and that included her sister.

The minute Avery got through the door, her son rushed her, extracting a more natural grin. It was hard not to smile when Andy was around.

"Hey, kiddo!" She ruffled his hair before wrapping her arms around him as he hugged her waist. She walked further into the kitchen without breaking contact. "You have school in the morning. Shouldn't you be in bed?"

"I was too scared to go to bed alone. Aunt Terry said I could wait up for you."

Avery hugged her son more fiercely. "Sorry I wasn't here, honey."

"That's okay. But I'll be able to sleep if you tuck me in."

Andy didn't wait for an answer, instead went skipping off toward his room with absolute conviction she would follow. Avery did, relieved he was so resilient, and wishing she could steal some of his resiliency. If only her mind worked like a child's, then she could forget the past and bounce back, ready to tackle the next phase of her life. Like a mantle, the shadow of her deeds fell on her shoulders again, weighing her down like the heaviest stones.

When she entered her son's room, Avery found him under the blanket, holding up a book and watching her with hopeful expectation. She grinned and strode toward him, unable to deny his unspoken request. Manipulated or not, she was a sucker for Andy's sweet expression.

She slid in next to him, got comfortable, and pulled him closer. With him curled beside her, she opened the book and began reading. Ten minutes later, she unwound herself from his slumbering form, careful not to wake him.

Avery stood and stared at her son's features, so much like Mike's. Raw pain gripped her, held her in its clutches, and ripped her heart in two. Andy was the spitting image of her husband at the same age. She had the many pictures in albums to prove it. Was this her punishment...to be haunted by her actions every time she looked at her son...never to forget?

Why had she sent that letter? Why hadn't she spoken up when she'd had the chance? Now it was too late. Would Andy forgive her if he knew? Avery sighed and tugged the blanket around him, more as a protective gesture than to keep him warm in the late May evening. She brushed a lock of dark hair off his forehead and smiled, still staring but no longer seeing her son's face.

Of course he'd never learn of it. She'd gone to great lengths to make sure. That last letter to Mike was now safely locked away from prying eyes, as was his answer. For some perverse reason, she'd saved both and kept going back to them night after night, as if she needed the reminder to never make the same mistake again. Sometimes she wished the military hadn't been so efficient in sending Mike's belongings back to her.

Her hand went to the heart-shaped locket she wore around her neck. Fingering the sweet gift Mike had sent her, she realized the memento was another reminder. Would she ever be able to take it off and move forward?

A tear broke loose, then trekked down her face. Where had her marriage gone wrong? Why hadn't she been able to love her husband enough for a lifetime? Now that her life was so jaggedly torn apart with his death, why did she wish she could undo what she'd done? *Because your letter most likely caused his death.*

Avery retreated from her son's room.

In the kitchen, Terry stood at the stove and lifted the whistling teakettle. The piercing sound died instantly. No one spoke.

She approached the counter noting two inviting cups and tea bags. "Just what I need."

"You looked a little frazzled." Terry spent a moment pouring hot water over the bags. Once done, she set the teakettle down before handing her the cup. "Figured you could use my calming remedy before I take off."

Avery's lips curled at the edges, forming the genuine smile that wouldn't come earlier. Terry's answer to every problem lay in a cup of tea—that and the accompanying conversation.

"Thanks," she murmured, lifting the cup to her lips. She leaned against the counter. Breathing in the aroma of the hot liquid, her smile increased. There might actually be some validity to the thinking, since she *was* feeling better.

"You shouldn't be skulking in cemeteries so close to dark. They aren't safe."

Avery almost choked on her tea. "I was visiting my dead husband's grave, not skulking. Besides, Arlington's an exception." No need to reveal how dangerous her visit had actually been.

The night's events had proven Arlington National Cemetery wasn't the safest place on earth, in fact had become a place to avoid, for now. Being shot at was enough to scare anyone senseless. She was safe and sound in her own kitchen. The danger had long passed. Now that the threat seemed far away, almost a distant memory, the idea somehow paled to the thought of being yanked to the ground by a stranger and then kissing him in a wild moment. A flush of heat streaked up her face. She quickly brought the tea closer to her mouth to camouflage her reaction. She and Terry shared secrets. Her sister even knew of Avery's request for a divorce from her husband, something no one else knew except her lawyer. She couldn't share this. Not yet.

If Terry caught wind of anything happening tonight, Avery would have to relay all the specifics…and quite frankly, she wasn't exactly sure what those specifics entailed. She certainly wouldn't be able to articulate so much as an inkling of what she'd been thinking. All she'd do is upset her sister. She had no idea why someone shot at her or even if she was the target.

Had to be him. As for the other? It was anyone's guess why an unknown man had drawn such a strong response, especially when her husband, whom she'd idolized as a teen and felt the luckiest person in the world to marry, never had. It had to be some kind of awkward response to her situation. Guilt and grief mixed with fear, resulting in an emotional overload.

"You look like you're feeling better. Your color's back." Terry shook her head and tsk-tsked like the older sister she was. "I just wish something more than a cemetery visit had caused it."

Avery's laugh, an indisputable burst of humor absent since before Mike's deployment to Afghanistan four months ago, felt natural. She took another long sip of tea. Then she exhaled, holding on to her smile. Maybe she was analyzing this from the wrong angle. Maybe the emotional overload from her near-death experience had been a good thing because suddenly she felt less encumbered. Freer. Something *had* happened tonight outside of the craziness of stray bullets and kissing strangers. Something inside her had changed, making her think of life beyond guilt.

She sighed. If only that were possible. She had no idea what the future held. All she knew was at that moment she felt…alive.

~~~

He'd begun tailing Avery Montgomery's car on her way out of the cemetery, following her until a few blocks from her house where he'd turned off and had circled back. He now sat half a block away, watching the house through binoculars.

All was calm. Upstairs, a few lights burned, revealing several open windows. He did a visual of the dark yard and noted a couple of tall trees. One might provide the means to get inside. Due to the earlier incident at the cemetery, tonight wasn't the time to try. She'd be wary and on her guard. He was thankful she hadn't called military police. That would have caused major headaches for all involved.

He rolled his eyes, wondering how this fucking operation had derailed so far off its original track. He didn't like putting innocent civilians at risk but the risk was necessary in this instance, according to his superiors. He started the car and pulled away from the curb.

He'd return at dawn and wait for an opportunity to search her house.

Amazon Link to The Sin Factor – http://amzn.to/SJvBlx

Made in United States
North Haven, CT
07 March 2023

33709707R00085